George Gresley Perry

The Life and Times of Robert Grosseteste

Bishop of Lincoln

George Gresley Perry

The Life and Times of Robert Grosseteste
Bishop of Lincoln

ISBN/EAN: 9783744687355

Printed in Europe, USA, Canada, Australia, Japan

Cover: Foto ©Raphael Reischuk / pixelio.de

More available books at **www.hansebooks.com**

THE LIFE AND TIMES

OF

ROBERT GROSSETESTE,

BISHOP OF LINCOLN.

*" Glorious is the fruit of good labours, and the root of wisdom shall
never fall away."—Wisdom iii. 15.*

BY

GEORGE G. PERRY, M.A.

PREBENDARY OF LINCOLN AND PROCTOR FOR THE DIOCESE.

Published under the Direction of the Tract Committee.

LONDON:
SOCIETY FOR PROMOTING CHRISTIAN KNOWLEDGE;
SOLD AT THE DEPOSITORIES:
77, GREAT QUEEN STREET, LINCOLN'S INN FIELDS;
4, ROYAL EXCHANGE; 48, PICCADILLY;
AND BY ALL BOOKSELLERS.
1871.

PREFACE.

THE sources from which the following Life of Bishop Grosseteste is principally taken are—1. A volume of the bishop's Latin letters, edited by Mr. Luard, with a valuable sketch of the Bishop's Life as preface. 2. The Chronicles or Annals of the Monasteries of Burton, Dunstable, Lanercost, and others. 3. A volume called "Monumenta Franciscana," containing the account of the Franciscans coming to England, and the letters of Adam de Marisco, an intimate friend of the bishop, edited by Mr. Brewer. 4. The " Greater History " of Matthew Paris, the Monk of St. Alban's. From this latter, as will be seen, the chief part of the incidents of Grosseteste's Life are taken. The famous Abbey of St. Alban's produced many valuable historical writers, of whom Matthew Paris, Roger of Wendover, and Thomas Walsingham, are perhaps the most renowned.

Matthew Paris also wrote another historical work, called " The Lesser History," and the greater part of the Chronicle called the "History of Matthew of Westminster," the other part of this having been composed by a Westminster monk, named John Bevere [1]. None of the Middle Age writers of our history is more interesting, and, for the most part, more trustworthy and fair, than Matthew Paris. But it must be remembered that as one of a body to whom Grosseteste was especially severe, he is inclined to bear rather hardly upon the bishop. On the other hand the bishop's opposition to Rome called forth his warm admiration, for Matthew Paris wrote in a thoroughly national spirit.

The following Life does not contain all that might be said about Bishop Grosseteste, but is chiefly confined to his work as a great reformer in a corrupt period of the Church, and to his quarrel with the Pope.

[1] Sir F. Madden's Preface to " Hist. Anglorum," p. 27.

THE LIFE AND TIMES

OF

ROBERT GROSSETESTE, BISHOP OF LINCOLN.

——◆——

CHAPTER I.

(INTRODUCTORY.)

The interest which attaches to Bishop Grosseteste's Life—As a great Church reformer—As the most learned man of his day—As taking a prominent part in a critical period of Public Affairs—His Life illustrative of the state of the Church of that period—The Monasteries—The Privileged Orders—The Parochial Clergy—The Chapter of Lincoln—Grosseteste not exempt from failings, but a noble and devoted character.

THE Life of Robert Grosseteste, the most famous bishop of the Mediæval Church of England, must needs interest all, who glory in connecting them-

selves with the old traditions of their country, and
love to think of their Church, not as a new Sect
sprung up in modern days, but as the lineal successor of the ancient Church of the land. Robert
Grosseteste was the Protestant of the thirteenth
century, but he was a Protestant upon the highest
Church principles, and from the conviction which
was forced upon him, that the Papal system, in its
practical working, was anti-Christian and destructive of souls. No man ever had more intense
faith in the divine mission of the Church. No
man ever made higher claims for Church authority.
No man was willing to concede more complete
ascendancy to him who claimed to be the Vicar of
Christ upon earth. But the evil use made by the
Pope of his pre-eminence revolted him, and stirred
his soul to utter those indignant protests with
which his life concludes. The most ardent supporter of Rome of his day, he died, if not excommunicated, yet cursed and reviled by the Pope.
This was because he loved the truth and right;
because his soul revolted from corruption and
deceit; because it refused to be contaminated, even
at the command of him, whom all his education
and habits of thought had taught him to regard as
the representative of God upon earth. Here was

a man whose zeal for holiness was the constraining influence of his life—a zeal not always according to knowledge, but always genuine and unpolluted. He lived in a corrupt age, and he aspired to be the great reformer of the Church of his day as his friend Simon de Montfort was of the State. He contended with monster abuses of all sorts, but he never ceased to combat bravely for the right. With the corrupted monasteries, with the ignorant and negligent clergy, with the unjust and encroaching king, with the Pope basely selling his edicts for gold,—he fought an unshrinking battle, and he did not fight in vain. The remembrance of his bold and earnest life animated many in after times who were called to the same struggles, and it may animate many yet to faithful labours for the truth.

Besides being the most ardent practical reformer Robert Grosseteste was also the most learned man of his time, not only in England, but in all Europe, and one of the most voluminous writers that England has produced. He was the greatest theologian, the greatest natural philosopher, the greatest master of language, of his day. His works, which are almost all still unprinted, are more than 200 in number, and are upon almost every subject of theology and science[1]. He wrote a religious poem in French, called "The Castle of Love," and is supposed to have written some other poems which are lost. He enjoyed the greatest reputation for learning of any man in his day, and preserved it all through the Middle Ages. For a writer to be able to quote *Lincolniensis* on his side was almost conclusive. John Wyclyffe in his controversies, constantly refers to him[2]. The good Bishop Hall rejoiced to be able to find a support for his scriptural views in this famous divine.

And if the interest which belongs to Bishop Grosseteste personally is so great, that which belongs to the era in which he lived is no less. His life commences before the beginning of the reign of John, and extends nearly up to the War of the Barons. It thus includes almost the whole period of the great struggle in this country for nationality in Church and State. The cause of

[1] The works of Bishop Grosseteste which are printed are a treatise on the "Ceasing of the Law," extracts from his Sermons and Lectures published by Mr. Brown in 1690, a collection of short scientific treatises published in the sixteenth century, and finally the valuable collection of his letters lately published by Mr. Luard.

[2] Lewis's Life of Wyclyffe, p. 3.

Church and State was essentially the same. To
both the great and pressing danger was the encroachments of aliens. John had basely consented
to hold his kingdom as a fief of the Pope, and the
Popes had not been slow to exercise the seignorial
rights which they had acquired. Pandulph, the
Pope's representative, had attempted to govern
England as a despotic governor in a subject province. The great minister, Hubert de Burgh, and
the noble Primate, Stephen Langton, had jointly
contended against, and at last overthrown him[3].
The Popes had treated the English Church as
that which they had a right to spoil and to dispose
of at their will; the Barons, the Commons, the
lower clergy, and, at length, the rulers of the State,
responded to their exactions by a resistance more
or less vigorous, which in the end triumphed in
the energetic hands of Edward 1. During the long
reign of Henry III. the feebleness and vacillation
of the king, his affection for foreigners, his pressing
need of money, and hence his inducement to court
the Pope, made the struggle for national independence difficult and fluctuating. The authority
of one Legate was overthrown, but Henry soon

[3] See Shirley's " Introduction to Royal and Historical Letters
of Henry III."

welcomed another to shield his weakness and to minister to his necessities. Archbishop Stephen Langton had put a stop to the Papal Provisions, which granted to foreigners benefices in the English Church, but in the times of Archbishop Edmund Rich this abuse became more flagrant than before. To Churchmen the Pope seemed to have a claim on their dutiful obedience as Head of the Church on earth.   He was able also to protect them from the king's exactions, and, from what appeared to them the most terrible of grievances, the subjection to the civil power.   Hence, in spite of many scandals and much injustice, Churchmen were inclined to cling to the Pope and to choose his side before that of the nation.   There were some indeed who took effectually the popular side, but generally the more influential clergy were for the Legates and the Pope, while the feeling of nationality and the desire for independence were stronger among the lower clergy and in the monasteries. Among those who at first ranged themselves distinctly on the Papal and foreign, and against the popular and national side, Robert Grosseteste occupies a conspicuous place.   " He was a Churchman of the highest hierarchical notions : Becket himself did not assert the immunities and privileges of

the Church with greater intrepidity[4]." He was
ready at all times to use his influence against the
king when he endeavoured to encroach upon or to tax
the Church.   He welcomed the Legate Otho.   At
Lyons he signed the rescript of King John's cession
of the kingdom to the Pope.   He gathered taxes
for the Pope.   He argued for the Pope's right
to dispose of all benefices.   He declined to join
the archbishop in opposing " Provisions."   Yet
he ended by denouncing the Pope's action in this
matter as in the highest degree iniquitous, and,
by appealing to the people of England to take their
stand on the nationality of their Church, and to
range the temporal power in its defence.   The life
of Grosseteste is, therefore, illustrative of the great
struggle of his day and of his century.   He commenced by boldly advocating the views to which,
by his antecedents and his surroundings, he was
altogether inclined, but the stern force of truth
and right compelled him at last to abandon them.
He commenced by welcoming the Legate, the
wielder of an irresponsible power; he ended by
excommunicating the breakers of Magna Charta,
and, had his life been prolonged, would probably
have energetically sided with the barons.   Even

4 Milman's " Latin Christianity," iv. 469.

more illustrative than of the public policy is the life of Grosseteste of the internal state of the Church of his time. And first, of the state of the monasteries:—

The writers of the twelfth century speak in the most bitter and melancholy tones of the demoralized state of the "religious" houses. They were pledged to follow the strict and searching rule of St. Benedict, but in almost all cases they utterly neglected it. If we may believe Walter Mapes, Archdeacon of Oxford in the twelfth century, the monks were for the most part given over to immorality[5]. St. Bernard, the most holy man of his day, and himself a monk, says that he is struck with amazement at the excesses in eating and drinking, in clothing, in bed-furniture, in equipages, to be seen every where in monasteries. "No one cares," he says, "for that bread which is from heaven; no attention is paid to the Scriptures or to the salvation of souls; jokes and merriment are all the care. During the feast as much as the jaws are occupied with eating, so are the ears with idle talk. Dishes are heaped upon dishes, and so great is the art of the cook that you may devour four or five and not be satisfied." The strongest wines

[5] Mapes' "Latin Poems," published by the Camden Society.

were carefully sought for and consumed to excess. The most delicate stuffs were procured for clothing. Abbots might be seen with a train of sixty horse, and all sorts of luxuries carried in their train[6]. The way of life prevailing in some English monasteries is clearly shown in some of their Chronicles recently published. In Dunstable Priory the whole effort of the canons seems to have been to gain possession of seignorial rights over the town, and sometimes by open violence, sometimes by legal quibbles, to get the advowsons of churches and the right to appropriate tithes. The monastery was bitterly hated by the townspeople. The Annals of Tewkesbury Abbey disclose the same sort of grasping and unfair tricks used to gain property and advowsons. The Chronicle of Evesham draws a picture of the grossest immorality prevailing in the abbey, and gives us plainly to understand that it was the general custom of the monks to forge documents. All these houses, without exception, held the bishop's visitation, to which they were subject, the most terrible of evils, and resorted to every sort of device to evade it. At Coventry the visitation was openly resisted and the prior suspended in consequence. The Abbots of St. Augus-

[6] "Apology to Abbot William."   Works of St. Bernard.

tine at Canterbury, of Edmundsbury, and Westminster were suspended on the same ground[7].
Now, with this corrupted state of the monasteries
Bishop Grosseteste resolutely set himself to grapple,
and by his zeal and energy he succeeded in pro-
ducing great reforms.   But he had the utmost difficulties to contend against.   Not only had he to
defeat the opposition and intrigues of those monasteries which were legally subject to his inspection,
but there was a great number of religious houses
which were specially exempted from all visitation
of the bishop, by privileges granted by the Pope.
The chief of these were the houses of the Cistercians,
or White Monks, an Order founded in the eleventh
century as a reform of the old Benedictines, or Black
Monks, by Robert, Alberic, and Stephen the Englishman, and to which Order the great St. Bernard
belonged.   The first house of this Order founded in
England was the Abbey of Waverly, near Farnham,
founded in 1120, but it spread so rapidly that almost
all the great monasteries built during the next 150
years belonged to it.   The Cistercians were at first
famous for their austerity, their hard work in the

---

[7] The Annals of almost all the abbeys mentioned have been
published in the series edited under the direction of the Master of
the Rolls.

fields, their severe mortifications in their houses, but they soon became very rich and luxurious. The splendid Abbeys of Furness, Rievaulx, Fountains, Tintern, and Vale Royal, belonged to the White Monks. In Grosseteste's time they much needed visitation, but they were fenced off from him by the privileges given them by the Popes. So great were these privileges that the Cistercian was bound by no law, human or divine, save his own rule. He might commit any crime: he might obstruct and paralyze ecclesiastical discipline; he might exempt large tracts from contributions to the burdens of the State; he might rob the parish priest of his dues, and none could inquire into his doings save the chief abbots of his own Order. This abuse and other similar ones attaching to the military Orders, the Templars and Hospitallers, Bishop Grosseteste set himself to overcome, and at last, with infinite trouble, succeeded in great measure in doing. Besides these great Exempt Orders, as they were called, there were in England in the days of Bishop Grosseteste numerous " cells," or small establishments of foreign monks, sent from some foreign monastery, and dependent only upon the mother establishment for discipline. These, as we shall see in the bishop's Life, were the most degraded and openly immoral of the misnamed religious houses, and gave him considerable trouble.

Nor was the state of the parochial clergy in the time of Bishop Grosseteste better than that of the monks. We have the strongest testimony that among the higher clergy the crime of simony, of taking bribes for every thing, was almost universal. The inquiries and directions published by the bishops of that day show us that immorality was abundantly prevalent, while Bishop Grosseteste's own Constitutions or rules for the conduct of his clergy, by the practices which they forbid, and the amount of knowledge which they describe as necessary in a clergyman, do not give us a high idea of the clerical state. Indeed the bishop describes, in words which will be quoted hereafter[8], a melancholy state of degradation in the clerical life, and this, as a monster abuse, he set himself with all his energy to reform. As his chief instrument for reforming the clergy, he trusted to the two great Orders of Dominican and Franciscan Friars, who were then in the first fervour of their zeal, and who numbered in their body some of the most noble spirits of the day. The interesting story of the first itroduction of the Franciscans into England, and of Grosse-

[8] See Chapter X.

teste's early connexion with them, will be told below. The bishop lived long enough, unfortunately, to see the falling off of those whom he had known in all the excellence of their first earnestness, and on his death-bed he condemned in solemn and severe tones the corruptions into which the friars were beginning to fall—a corruption which eventually was far more complete than even that of the monks. There was yet one other great difficulty with which Bishop Grosseteste had to contend in his labours for reforming the Church; this was the special privileges and immunities of the Chapter of his own cathedral. In the life of St. Hugh, the famous Burgundian[9], who built the cathedral of Lincoln, we read that the Canons of that church affected the state and pomp, as they had the revenues, of feudal lords. We are also told that they despised Bishop Grosseteste on account of his low origin[1]. Accordingly they refused to allow him either to exercise a visitation in the cathedral, or in any of the numerous churches which were affiliated to it. This, as subversive of discipline, the bishop stoutly resisted, and after a long and costly struggle, in which the characters of all concerned somewhat suffered, he was successful.

---

[9] Published in the Rolls Series.   [1] Matthew Paris.

It will be seen, then, that Bishop Grosseteste was an uncompromising reformer and a great beater-down of ecclesiastical abuses. It will be seen also that in doing this he often used questionable means, and showed himself deficient in temper, judgment, and fairness. But though he was often wrong in the means which he employed, he never for a moment faltered in his devotion to that which was the great object of his life—the purifying and strengthening of the Church, and the setting forward the salvation of souls. Every aberration which he seems to have made from the right path will be plainly stated; but the main character of this noble life will not be affected by them. From infirmities of nature, from errors of judgment, he was not exempt, but these are but trifling blemishes which do not impair the substantial beauty of this life so full of unselfish earnestness and true Christian love.

CHAPTER II.

GROSSETESTE AS SCHOLAR.

1175—1225.

Place of Grosseteste's birth—His name—A Student at Oxford—State of Oxford in his time—The Hospices or Halls—The Schools—Oxford Studies—Grosseteste goes to Paris—Is recommended as Secretary to the Bishop of Hereford—Giraldus Cambrensis at Oxford—Grosseteste returns thither and reaches great eminence for learning—Mention of him by Gower—by Robert de Brune—His Studies of Greek—of Hebrew—The Jews in England—His French Poem, "The Castle of Love"—His scientific works—His theological works.

As is the case with many men who have made themselves a great name, Robert, the famous English bishop of the thirteenth century, was <u>born</u> <u>in obscurity,</u> and round his early years much darkness hangs. His birth is usually assigned to the year 1175, and, as this date best agrees with some ascertained periods of his after life, we may assume it to be correct. The place of his birth is somewhat more clearly indicated. Nicholas Trivet, the chronicler, speaks of him as born in Suffolk, in the Diocese of Norwich, and the Chronicle which passes under the name of Matthew of Westminster, mentions Stradbrook, as the place of his birth. The rhyming Chronicle of Richard of Bardney, which assigns his birth to Stow in Lincolnshire, may be dismissed as inaccurate as regards his birth-place, but it is not so clear that the Bardney monk was wrong in his assertion as to the early connexion of Robert with Lincoln as a scholar. Giraldus the famous Welsh scholar who lived about Grosse-teste's time, speaks of a good school at Lincoln, under a very famous master, Wilhelmus de Monte, and says that he himself had studied under him and left his school with regret[1]. It is possible that at this school Robert may have been taught, as Richard of Bardney states.

That he came of a peasant family may be accepted as certain. Trivet declares him to come of the "very lowest race." The "Lanercost Chronicle," the composition of Franciscan friars,

[1] "Giraldus Cambrensis," Ed. Brewer, i. 93, 110.

and most friendly to Grosseteste, says, that "in family indeed he was most low[2]," and the reproach put by Matthew Paris into the mouths of the Canons of Lincoln as to the lowness of his origin seems decisive on the point.   As a son of a peasant, without landed estate, Robert would have no family name,—the name which he afterwards acquired being doubtless due to the peculiarity of his personal appearance, the largeness of his head. Matthew Paris speaks of him as " Robert who is known by the surname of Grosseteste," or " Robert called Great-Head."   Nicholas Trivet says, " he was surnamed by many Great-Head."   And Robert of Brune, who at the beginning of the fourteenth century versified in English William of Wadington's "Manuel des Pechiez," says, " His *to-name* is Grosseteste."   Anthony Wood reckons up no less than twelve different ways of expressing his title, and at the same time observes that in Latin works written by English men he is generally called Capito, whereas foreigners often quote him as Rupertus, and he is also frequently distinguished simply as Lincolniensis.   In the romancing poem of Richard of Bardney he is represented as coming in a destitute and ragged condition to beg at the

[2] " Chron. Lanercost," p. 43.

door of the Mayor of Lincoln, and refusing to accept alms on the condition that he would undertake never to be bishop of the See. He departs, and the mayor sends after him to press alms upon him, but the squalid youth expresses his contempt for bodily food, and declares that he was only begging for means to enable him to enter the school which flourished at Lincoln. Of course the mayor procures him an admission, and, equally of course, he soon distances all competitors. It would not be worth while to allude to this monkish romance were it not probable to some extent on other grounds that Robert may have been first taught at Lincoln. His close and intimate acquaintanceship with Hugh de Welles, Bishop of Lincoln, which was the cause of all his promotions, brings early connexion with Lincoln at least within the range of probability. But whether he received his earliest instruction under the shade of the minster just then rising to its glory through the pious and skilful munificence of St. Hugh, or not, it is certain that Robert was soon attracted to the great central school of England—the University of Oxford.

The time when he went to Oxford to study must have been towards the end of the twelfth century.

At this period Oxford studies had undergone a transformation, which seriously affected the schools established there as places of training for the young student. The division of the subjects of study into Trivials and Quadrivials[3] which had prevailed ever since the revival of learning under Charlemagne, and had governed the studies of Europe, had now for some time fallen into disrepute. Men had learned to apply themselves to special studies, law, physic, and divinity, especially to the former, by the knowledge of which they were able to obtain a lucrative compensation for their labours[4]. Paying more regard to the subject than to the style, their Latinity began to suffer, and barbarisms to increase and abound. Thémes and scholarly exercises were laid aside for ingenious and subtle disputations on topics of law and divinity. The famous collection of Sentences made by Peter Lombard had set all the wits of Europe trying to solve hard problems of casuistry and theology, and to be one of the " Scholars " of the Master was now the rage among those who aspired to literary

[3] The Trivials were Grammar, Rhetoric, and Logic; the Quadrivials, Arithmetic, Music, Geometry and Astronomy.

[4] Wood's " Annals of Oxford," i. 157, 159, 161, 168. Brewer's " Introd. to Bacon," p. xviii.

fame[5]. It is said that this change in the studies of English clerks, caused the migration of many who were dissatisfied with it from England to Philip, King of France, who received them readily, and founded for them the English College at Paris. " Hence," says Anthony Wood, " dotages and corruptions in learning " were secretly imported into England, and many "halting and foolish opinions were foisted into our schools[6]." Probably this period was one of the darkest in the literary history of Oxford. The young unknown Suffolk peasant who came now to take up his abode at the University, was destined to do more than any man of his day to raise the character of Oxford for learning. By the mere force of his own genius, as it would seem, and owing but little to any helps to be found in his place of study,—discarding the miserable translations of Aristotle, which, as Roger Bacon shows, were more likely to mislead than to teach[7]—taking the way of original thought and experiment,—Robert obtained from the voices of all his contemporaries the reputation of a most consummate philosopher.

[5] Hence the term " Scholastic Divinity," and " Schoolmen."
[6] " Annals," i. 164, 5.
[7] Brewer's " Bacon," p. 469.

The time of his arrival at Oxford was at least fifty years antecedent to the foundation of the earliest of the colleges. St. Frydeswyde's and Osney Abbey were the only great foundations in existence, and these were only indirectly connected with the University as a place of learning. With the thirteenth century, the history of Oxford commences; all before this is vague conjecture, and no documents are in existence to give us any definite knowledge of an earlier date[8]. What, then, was the University as it was displayed to the young Suffolk peasant, with that great capacity and deep thirst for learning of his, when he saw it in the early days of King John? The most ancient document in existence, bearing upon the history of Oxford, is a letter of the Pope's legate, in which he inflicts, as a punishment upon the citizens of Oxford, the obligation to charge half rent only for all the Hospices let to clerks in that city[9]. These Hospices, " Inns " or " Entries," at first without any check or control, were by very early statutes of the University to be kept of necessity by a

---

[8] " Munimenta Academica," Ed. Anstey; Introd., p. 33. In his most interesting Introduction to the valuable work which he has edited for the Master of the Rolls, Mr. Anstey has given as good a sketch as can probably be made of mediæval Oxford.

[9] " Munimenta Academica," p. 1.

graduate, who paid the rent to the burgess for the building, and a certain tax to the general fund of the University for the privilege to take in scholars. The principal officer of the University, called the Chancellor, or Master of the Scholars, had the right of depriving any keeper of a hospice of his licence, and by his authority he enforced upon them certain disciplinary arrangements. The greatest number of these hospices which existed at any time, was about eighty[1], and after the fire of Oxford, in 1190, these were mostly built of stone and tiles. Inasmuch, however, as this was a new fashion, these buildings of extra solidity were called "stone halls" or "tiled halls," while at the same time there existed along side of them the more humble buildings of ancient construction[2].

Robert probably entered at one of small pretensions as his slender means would incline him. As yet there were none but chance provisions or helps for poor scholars, the excellent provisions of "chests" (or banks for lending money on deposit) being established by Grosseteste himself afterwards, when he had grown in age and influence. Having found a footing in one of the hospices or halls, the

----

[1] "Munimenta Acad.," p. 48.
[2] Wood, "Annals," i. 172.

next thing for the young scholar to do was to
select the school or schools in which he was to hear
lectures and perform disputations. As every
Master of Arts was an *Inceptor*, or competent to
commence lecturing, and bound to do so, the number
of professors was very great. These were accom-
modated for the purposes of their lectures in the
thirty-two schools to be found in School-street,
and in the other buildings of like character in the
city. It seems that clerks had a right of demanding any house from its owner for this use, and
renting it at a certain salary fixed by regular
valuers.[3] The younger boys meanwhile were provided for at grammar-schools, the teachers of
which occupied a position subordinate to the in-
ceptors, and were not always members of the
University. Both in the grammar-schools and in
those of a higher class, there was a distinction
between those strictly belonging to the University
and those who belonged to religious houses (St.
Frydeswyde, Osney, Eynsham, &c.) teaching
within the University, and subject to its general
rules. This privilege, allowed to the religious
bodies, proved a very important one when the
active Orders of the Mendicant Friars became

---

[3] "Munimenta Academica," Introd. p. 49.

established at Oxford. Soon the Dominicans, Franciscans and Austins[4], gained the highest reputation for learning, and carried off the chief honours of the place. But when Grosseteste entered Oxford no friars were as yet in England, and he himself was destined to be the chief means of raising the Franciscan school to eminence. Having found a hall and a school, what would the Oxford student of the twelfth century compass thereby as food for his mental cravings? He would get, first of all, a positive and formal instruction in Latin parsing. He would have verses and themes to write and to learn to repeat by heart. He would have to master his Priscian and Donatus, and to learn to illustrate the rules from Ovid, being at the same time able to translate this favourite author both into English and French[5]. Having gone through this preliminary training, the scholar advanced to become an " artist," would have to attend lectures on the Trivials and Quadrivials, being himself frequently questioned and having to answer[6], and at length to undergo a more formal

---

[4] They were especially famous for Grammar.

[5] The expression of a " boy in his Ovid " is used by Grosseteste when he wishes to rebuke the nomination of a youthful student to a living.

[6] Hence the term " Responsions " came to be applied to the

ordeal in the *parvise*. At so very early a date as
that of Grosseteste's entrance at Oxford, University
life had not acquired the form and regularity with
which we find it invested a hundred years later;
but, doubtless, there must have been masters to
lecture and scholars to hear. In the earliest record
of University doings which we possess, we hear
of some sturdy masters who insisted on continuing
to read their lectures after the others had fled, and
thus incurred the animadversion of the Legate.
The same document also informs us what would
be considered a good dinner for a scholar in
those days (1214), namely, bread, ale, soup, and
one dish of fish or flesh.

That Grosseteste went from Oxford to Paris there
can be no reasonable doubt, inasmuch as the historian of the University of Paris speaks confidently
as to his presence and his doings there[7]. Further,
we know that it was the custom in his day for all
the Oxford scholars who were zealous to improve
themselves, to resort to that great head-quarters of
learning; and we have in one of Grosseteste's own

preliminary examination; and, as this seems to have been held
originally in a "priest's chamber," *parvisum*, the "in parviso
respondentes," has survived to our own day.

7 "Bulæus," vol. iii. S.V.

letters a reference to the studies of Paris, which may seem to decide the matter[8]. Bulæus says, "Robertus, surnamed Capito, for a long period studied letters in this University, and obtained here all the Master's degrees;" and in another place he calls him, "formerly an illustrious professor in the University of Paris." The young scholar's travelling expenses to Paris, and his support when there, may have been procured in the same way that Edmund Rich procured his[9], namely, by asking alms; and we may be sure that these charitable contributions were well bestowed, and that the indefatigable student let no opportunity slip of making advances in the studies he loved so much. It is probable that at Paris he laid the foundation of his knowledge of Greek and Hebrew. In Greek it is most likely that he had the instruction of Nicholas the Greek, who, according to Wood, had formerly taught at Oxford, and afterwards at Paris[9]. Matthew Paris records the fact that the translation of the Testaments of the Twelve Patriarchs which Grosseteste made, or procured to be made, was done by the assistance of Nicholas, whom he describes as a clerk of the Abbot of St.

[8] Epist. 124. Luard, p. 346.
[9] Dr. Hook's "Lives of the Archbishops," iii. 137.

Alban's[1].   If this were so, it is most probable that the bishop had an earlier knowledge of Nicholas as a teacher of the language.

We now come to what is really the first contemporary notice of one who was afterwards to fill so large a space in the Chronicles and Annals of his country.   About the year 1200 the famous divine, historian, and topographer, Giraldus de Barry, better known as Giraldus Cambrensis, wrote a letter to William de Vere, Bishop of Hereford, to recommend to him a young scholar who would be useful to him in his household, and in all the various matters with which a bishop had to deal.   The letter ran as follows: " He who interposes for good men is (as Symmachus tells us,) not more advancing their interests than commending his own judgment.   On this ground I merely wish to suggest to your discretion with regard to Master Robert Grosseteste, whom, as I have gladly heard, you have lately received into your family, that the reward he obtains from you should equal his merits. For I know that his help in your various affairs, in your decisions of causes, and in the care of your bodily health, will soon be made doubly, ay, manifoldly necessary to you.   For in his case those powers

[1] S. A. 1242.

which in these our days are wont to be beyond all others profitable in temporal things, have been raised upon the firm foundation of the liberal arts, and a copious acquaintance with books, and are illustrated and adorned by a most excellent moral character. It is often the case that those who are skilled in the faculties which I have mentioned are weak in the matter of trustworthiness; but I may say of Robert, that, beyond all the rest of the good qualities in which he excels, he is conspicuous in trustworthiness and fidelity. And to put into a few words a great mass of praise, I know him to be of such a disposition and of such industry that you will find in him a man after your own heart, and one in whom your spirit will receive very good repose[2]." Now, how did the learned Welshman gain such a knowledge of the Oxford clerk as to be able to recommend him so strongly and confidently? Not long before this letter was written Giraldus had visited Oxford, fired with the ambition of rivalling the Father of History, and of reciting in the ears of a learned audience the great work which he had recently completed, on the "Topography of Ireland." This work was divided into three distinctions, or parts, to the recital of each of which

[2] Wharton's "Anglia Sacra," ii. 344.

a day was assigned. He has himself described what took place at the recitation. "In process of time when the work was completed, not willing to hide his candle under a bushel, but to place it on a candlestick, that it might give light to all, he resolved to read it publicly in Oxford, where the most learned and famous of the English clergy were at that time to be found. And as there were three distinctions or divisions in the work, and each division occupied a day, the readings lasted three successive days. On the first day he received and entertained at his lodgings all the poor of the town; on the next day all the doctors of the different faculties, and such of their pupils as were of fame and note; on the third day the rest of the scholars, with the knights, townsmen, and many burgesses. It was a costly and noble act, because the authentic and ancient times of poesy were thus in some measure renewed, and neither present nor past can furnish any record of such solemnity ever having taken place in England [3]." The visit of Giraldus to Oxford and the pretentious proceedings in which he

---

[3] Brewer's "Giraldus Cambrensis," Preface, p. 47. See also A. Wood's "Annals of Oxford," S. A. 1200. In Mr. Brewer's Preface will be found an excellent account of the " Topographia Hiberniae."

indulged, making him acquainted, as they naturally would with all the notabilities of the place, may have very well been the means of bringing to his notice the young Suffolk scholar Robert, lately returned with a high reputation from Paris, where Giraldus had also studied. Grosseteste may have gone to Hereford intent upon carrying out, as far as his influence with the bishop would allow him, those schemes of Church reform which were perhaps already in his mind. But, whatever were his desires and motives in entering the household of the Bishop of Hereford, they were not destined to be realized or to produce any lasting effect at that time. The bishop died very soon after Grosseteste had come to him, and the young scholar returned to Oxford to resume his studies, which he was now to carry on with but little interruption for the next thirty years of his life.

At what time after his return to Oxford from the house of the Bishop of Hereford, Grosseteste reached the dignity of *Rector-Scholarum* in the University, it is hard to say; but that he did reach and hold for some time this office there is satisfactory evidence[4]. The Rector Scholarum was

<hr>

[4] Luard, "Grosseteste Ep." Pref. p. 33.

otherwise described as Chancellor, (holding perhaps, a somewhat similar office to the Vice-Chancellor of more modern times,) and it was without doubt the most eminent office in the University. Grosseteste is also said to have graduated in Divinity, then a novel practice at Oxford, Archbishop Edmund Rich, his contemporary, having been the first who bore the title of Doctor of Divinity[5]. That the fame of Grosseteste at Oxford as a scholar, and teacher, was of the very highest order, we have abundant evidence. John Tyssyngton says of him: "To compare him to the modern doctors is as the comparison of the sun to the moon when it is eclipsed[6]." Roger Bacon, his contemporary, perhaps his pupil, has left numerous records of the high estimation in which he held his learning; and so great was his fame that, like other learned men of that age, he was usually held to be a practiser of magic.

This popular fancy we find embodied in John Gower's verse :—

> " For of the grete clerk Grostest
> I rede how redy that he was,
> Upon clergy an hede of brass
> To make and forge it for to telle

---

[5] Hook's " Archbishops," iii. 144.
[6] Wood, " Annals," i. 202.

> Of such thyngs as befelle;
> And seven yeres besinesse
> He layde but for the lacklesse
> Of halfe a mynute of an houre,
> Fro fyrst that he began laboure
> He lost al that he had do [7]."

The "head of brass" is usually attributed to Roger Bacon, but it seems that Grosseteste also had to bear the popular suspicion for his learning. Another poetical testimony to the fame of the great scholar is furnished us by the Gilbertine canon, Robert de Brune, early in the fourteenth century :—

> " I shall tell, as I have herd,
> Of the byshop Saint Roberd;
> His toname is Grossteste,
> Of Lyncolne, so seyth the geste :
> He loved moche to here the harpe,
> For mannes wit it makyth sharpe;
> Next hys chamber, besyde hys study
> Hys harper's chamber was fast the by.
> Many tymes, by nightes and dayes,
> He hadd solace of notes and layes.
> On asked hyme the reason why
> He had delyte in mynstrelsy;
> He answered hym in this manere
> Why he held the harpe so dere :
> The virtu of the harpe, through skyll and ryght,
> Will destrye the fendy's myght;
> And to the cros, by gode skeyl,
> Ys the harpe lykened well [8]."

---

[7] Gower, "Confess. Amantis," b. iv.
[8] Robert de Brune, "Handlyng Synne."

The great renown of Grosseteste as a scholar is emphatically testified by Nicholas Trivet, in his Chronicle, who also enumerates some of the special subjects of his studies. "He was," says the chronicler, "a man of excellent wisdom, and of most lucid power of teaching, as well as a pattern of all virtue. The good abilities which he had from nature he cultivated by the precepts of Scripture, so as to form a noble soul. When he was Master of Arts he wrote briefly upon the ' Book of Posterior Analytics.'   He also put forth treatises on the ' Sphere,' the ' Art of Reckoning,' and many other things useful in philosophy. He was a doctor skilled in three tongues, the Latin, the Hebrew, and the Greek; and many things did he bring forth from the tongue of the Hebrews and caused many to be translated from the Greek[9]." The expression "caused to be translated" leads us to infer that Grosseteste, in the infancy of the knowledge of their then newly imported Greek, did not know the language sufficiently to translate by himself. And this in fact is asserted of him by Roger Bacon, both with regard to Greek and Hebrew. "The Greek and Hebrew he did not know sufficiently to translate them unassisted, but

[9] Trivet in " Dacherii Spicilegio," vii. 397.

he had many assistants[1]." Probably at this time Grosseteste's chief labour in Greek translation was on the books of Aristotle. Bacon indeed, in that admirable passage in which he speaks so eloquently of the advantages of studying philosophical works in the original rather than in the wretched translations then current, which he so bitterly condemns[2], says that Grosseteste (on account of these bad translations) " altogether neglected the books of Aristotle;" but this doubtless referred to the physical treatises. We know that he was familiar with the " Ethics," the " Analytics," and other works of Aristotle, and we may infer that he both studied them in the original, and assisted in translating them. An intellect like that of Grosseteste would feel all the force of the topics urged by Bacon, and appreciate the enthusiasm which makes him say, "Oh how delightful is the taste of wisdom to those who are thus steeped in it from its very fount and origin. They who have not tried this cannot feel the delight of wisdom, just as a sick man cannot estimate the flavour of food. But because they are affected with this sort of mental sickness, and their intellect in this matter is as it

---

1 Bacon, " Compend. Studii," c. viii.
2 " Comp. Studii," c. viii.

were deaf from their very birth, so as not to appreciate the delight of harmony, on this account they grieve not at this so great loss of wisdom, though indeed without doubt it is an infinite loss[3]." We must certainly assign then the earnest study of Greek, and of those noble models of the language found in the works of Aristotle, as part of Grosseteste's labours at Oxford. It was long after this that, deluded by misrepresentations, and not sufficiently versed in criticism to be able to see through them, he lent himself to the translation of that curious fiction, " The Testaments of the Twelve Patriarchs," and of that other strange and fanciful production, " The Hierarchy of Dionysius." His translation of this latter is believed still to exist, although, as more than one version was made of the book, it is not quite certain how much of the existing translation was actually made by the bishop.

The only other known translations made by Grosseteste from the Greek are some corrections and retranslations of the book of John of Damascus, "De Orthodoxâ Fide," and a legendary history of the Virgin Mary, of the date of the Emperor Justinian. His zeal to give a Latin dress to books of so little

[3] Bacon, "Comp. Stud.," c. viii.   Brewer's "Bacon," p. 466.

value as some of those which have been mentioned, may well lead us to suppose that he would not have failed to employ himself upon Aristotle, whom he prized so highly, if any Greek MSS. of his works came to his hands while at Oxford or Paris. But both Trivet and Roger Bacon speak of Grosseteste as not only making, or procuring to be made, translations from the Greek, but also from the Hebrew. Indeed Hebrew was better known at that period in England than Greek, and the instruction in it was more readily come at. William the Conqueror had permitted great numbers of Jews to come over from Rouen and to settle in England, about the year 1087. They increased rapidly, and spread themselves through the various towns of England, where they built synagogues. In the year 1189 there were no less than 1500 at York. At Bury, in Suffolk, there was a synagogue. By this means the learned became acquainted with their language and books. In the reign of William Rufus the Jews were especially numerous at Oxford, and had acquired a considerable property, and some of their Rabbis were allowed to open a school in the University, where they instructed not only their own people but Christian students also. Within 200 years after their first admission into England they were generally banished, and this caused a vast number of their books to fall into the hands of the clergy and monks[4]. We can thus easily trace the path by which Grosseteste would gain instruction in Hebrew and assistance in translating from it, and we have abundant proof that the interest which he took in the Jews was great and lasting. His book on the "Ceasing of the Law[5]" was written, doubtless, to endeavour to accomplish their conversion, and his letters on the occasion of the establishment of the House of the Converts manifest much more kindly feelings towards them than were then usually prevalent in England. Before quitting the subject of Grosseteste as a student of languages, we must touch upon his acquaintance with French; for French must have been to him an acquired tongue. The son of a Suffolk peasant, he could not have been familiar with it as spoken in England, until he began to mix among persons of higher station. Yet as a proof of the prevalence of the French

[4] "Anglia Judaica," quoted by Warton, "Dissert.," ii. Gregory, Prior of Ramsey, and Roger Bacon are specially noted as acquirers of Hebrew MSS.

[5] This book was printed in an imperfect form by Dr. Bruno Ryves in the year 1658. The MS. of the whole treatise is in Trin. Coll. Camb. Library.

tongue at that day in England, it is very noteworthy that in the poem which he composed in French, Grosseteste prefaces by an apology in Latin: "And although the romance tongue has not for clerks any savour of sweetness, yet, for the laity, who understand less, this little work is suitable."

The name by which the poem is called, "Castle of Love," refers to the Incarnation described in the poem, the castle being the body of the Blessed Virgin. It was translated into English early in the fourteenth century, and several versions of it exist. Under a curious imagery and strange conceits, it is intended to give the unlearned a general résumé of the chief facts of Scripture. There are many other mediæval poems of a similar character, both in old French and old English, and one cannot but regard the object of them to have been excellent,—nor doubt that by their means a very considerable amount of Scriptural knowledge was spread abroad. When we see in Grosseteste's Latin works the intense love and devotion which he had for the Holy Scriptures, we can well understand his interrupting his numerous labours, and breaking in upon his abstract studies to write this simple doggerel for the sake of the unlearned, in whose minds he desired to see fixed the great truths of Holy Writ.

We come now to consider that part of Grosseteste's studies on which his great reputation among his contemporaries, and throughout the Middle Ages, was principally based,—his philosophical, or as we should say, physical studies.   Roger Bacon says of him emphatically: "He alone of himself knew all sciences [6];" and again, "The Lord Robert neglected altogether the books of Aristotle and their methods, and by his own experiments and other helps, employed himself in those scientific matters which Aristotle had treated," and "he understood and wrote of those things concerning which the books of Aristotle speak."   And again, "The Lord Robert alone, of account of his long life, and the wonderful methods which he used, before all other men knew the sciences [7]."   It is plain enough that Bacon grounds the fame of Grosseteste upon his physical studies, and in fact the treatises to which he especially refers as being so remarkable, are those on the rainbow and comets.   Trivet instances those on the sphere and the calendar, and "many other things in philosophy."   Giraldus Cambrensis, in

[6] "Opus Tertium," c. xii.
[7] "Comp. Studii," c. viii.   Brewer, 469, 472.

the letter given above, commendatory of Grosseteste, mentions his skill in medicine as his chief
recommendation. It was just in Grosseteste's day
that natural science, by way of observation and
experiment, began to dawn. In his love of this
Grosseteste was the precursor of Roger Bacon and
of some of the earlier friars[8]. Mens' minds, wearied
with the old stale dogmata, accepted with eagerness the notion of discovering the truth by experimental investigation. To experiment Grosseteste
doubtless gave himself, and hence Gower's story
about the brazen head, and Bacon's expression
about the " wonderful methods " which he used.
The catalogue of his works exhibits treatises on
sound, motion, heat, colour, form, angles, atmos-
pheric pressure, poison, the rainbow, comets, light;
as well as on the astrolabe, the philosopher's stone,
necromancy, and witchcraft. There was, indeed,
no part of astronomy, chemistry, metallurgy, or
mechanics, where elucidation was not attempted by
this universal genius, and in which, in the judg-

[8] " With the Friars came the first systematic attention to
medical studies, and to natural philosophy in general. . . There
is scarcely a writer among them, distinguished as he may be for
logical and metaphysical ability, who is not equally interested in
experimental philosophy."   Brewer, Introd. to " Monumenta
Franciscana," p. 43.

ment of his contemporaries, he did not achieve great success. He too, like Roger Bacon, wrote a *Compendium of Sciences*, containing in its twenty books a sort of universal instruction, and thus anticipated some of the credit which is most justly given to Bacon[9]. Doubtless Grosseteste had more means at hand for his work than Bacon, the Franciscan friar, who was interdicted from books, and obliged to contend against numerous artificial obstacles; but the charge of witchcraft was not sparingly used against Grosseteste also, and as the first to tread this original path, he had in some ways need of more self-reliance and genuine courage than even Bacon himself. As a vast encyclopædia of learning, Grosseteste stood forth as the wonder of his age, and challenges the admiration of posterity. And when it is remembered that the multitudinous works which he composed were the productions, not of a cloistered recluse, but of a man actively engaged throughout his time, first as a teacher and lecturer at Oxford, and then as the energetic bishop of the largest See in England, we stand in amazement at his labours.

But in glancing at Grosseteste's scientific works we have only indicated one division of his pro-

<hr>

[9] Preface to " Opera inedita," p. 57.

ductions. In theology he was even more prolific
than in science. The " Chronicle of Lanercost,"
which supplies several particulars of his life, says,
" He postilled the Psalter as far as the middle,"
and leaves its readers to infer that this was the
only or chief work of the bishop's in divinity.
But the lists of the bibliographers give us the titles
of between two and three hundred of his sermons,
between sixty and seventy of his larger treatises,
besides the collections of Dicta, or "Sayings," which
contain 147 short discourses. Were the theological works of Grosseteste all printed, they would
fill several large folio volumes[1]. And it is very
noteworthy that absolutely none of them were
printed until very long after the invention of the
art, while the works of other and very inferior
writers were sought out and carefully set forth in
type.

And yet his theological teaching, judging from
what has been printed, is eminently worthy of
greater attention. " It is a remarkable thing,"
says Brown, "and not to be lightly passed by,
that the memory of this man has so long remained

---

[1] This was ascertained by Archbishop Williams, who, when
Bishop of Lincoln, began the task of collecting Grosseteste's
works.

fragrant when so few of his works, and those not of the greatest value, are extant. Men who are zealous for the truth seem to be challenged to seek out and publish what he in his lifetime wrote with such spirit and labour. What trash of worthless writers loads our bookshops and libraries, when far more useful writings are kept in prison and darkness on account of the idleness of men who will not put a hand to bring them forth[2]." Probably the greater part of the sermons remaining in MS. were preached by Grosseteste after he had reached the episcopal rank, but the " Sayings " have the appearance of having been delivered as lectures at Oxford; and generally they are plain, simple and powerful applications of Scripture truths, with great force of illustration and terseness of language. The reverence for Scripture is unbounded, and no authority of Church, or Pope, or Councils, is put upon the same platform as the authority of Holy Writ. " Faith," says Grosseteste, " is the assent of our thoughts by means of some medium. The medium which ought to produce the greatest faith is the authority of Sacred Scripture. Those things, therefore, which are of faith, are especially those to which we assent on the authority of Holy

2 " Fasciculus," ii.245.

Scripture; so that, more properly, faith may be said to be the belief of those things which are believed by the authority of Holy Scripture[3]." In speaking of prayer, not a word is said as to praying to or through the saints. "Those good things which we want cannot be given except by the grace of God through Jesus Christ our Lord; wherefore they are to be sought for from God alone. Nor ought we to doubt that He will give them, inasmuch as He spared not His only Son, but gave Him for us all[4]." A passage on united prayer may serve as a specimen of Grosseteste's method of illustration. "That is a good thing which is not diminished by the distribution of itself, but is only made the more delightful in proportion as it is joined in by more. As many heavy things when bound together descend the quicker, and many light things when united ascend with more velocity, inasmuch as the inclination of each of the separate things has a general effect upon the mass; so many individuals joined together by the bond of love and prayer, are moved upwards more easily and more swiftly, the virtue of the prayer of each having an effect upon each. For like polished

---

[3] Dictum de Fide. Fascic. ii. 281.
[4] Dictum de Orando.   Fascic. ii. 283.

bodies, when placed close together and illuminated by the power of the sun, in proportion to their number, shine the more on account of the multitude of the reflections of the rays of light, so the more souls that are illuminated by the rays of the sun of righteousness shine the more on account of the reflection of mutual love[5]." His definitions of various virtues and vices are thoughtful and striking. Pride is "an inordinate fondness of one's own excelling." Envy, "an inordinate fondness of the depression of another." Humility is the "love of remaining firmly in the place fitting to one under all conditions." Patience is "the inflexibility of the soul as respects troubles." His words on the union of divine grace and human will in action are admirable. "Every thing which is in us is from the grace of God, for there is no good thing which He does not wish to be, and His will is the cause of being. There is no good thing, therefore, which He does not make. The aversion of the will from evil, its conversion to good, its perseverence in good, He makes. Nevertheless, these same things our free will also makes, just as the grain of corn germinates by a kind of germinative power which is exterior to it, by the heat of the

---

[5] Dictum de Orando. Fascic. ii. 284.

sun and the moisture of the earth.   For if we could not turn ourselves away from evil and turn ourselves to good, we should not deserve praise for this, nor in Scripture should we be enjoined so to do.   And if we could do this without grace, God would not need to be prayed for this, nor would His will be the doing of it[6]."

[6] Dictum de Gratiâ.   Fascic. ii. 284.

CHAPTER III.

GROSSETESTE AS TEACHER.

1225—1235.

Grosseteste made Teacher to the Franciscan Friars at Oxford—The History of the first settlement of these Friars in England—They are instructed in Preaching by Grosseteste—The Sermons of that day— Grosseteste's various Preferments given by Bishop Hugh de Welles—His scruples about holding them —Projects and abandons a visit to Italy—Resigns his Preferments—His letter to his sister Juetta— to his friend Adam Marsh—to a clergyman of vicious life—His deep religious impressions.

THAT Grosseteste's lectures and discourses on Scriptural subjects must have been in the highest degree valuable cannot be doubted; and well indeed did those who had the direction of the great revival movement of the thirteenth century—the establishment of the Friars,—judge, when, as one of the first steps for promoting the work of the Franciscans in England, they engaged Grosseteste to be their teacher in theology at Oxford. But it will not perhaps be unfit to digress here for a moment to show how the Franciscans reached Oxford at this particular time.

It was in the year 1224 that the first detachment of the Franciscan Minorite, or Grey Friars, whose zeal and devotion were already edifying Europe, reached England[1]. They landed at Dover, being nine in number, four clerks and five laymen. The leader of the party was Agnellus of Pisa, who had been chosen by St. Francis as the provincial minister for England. He was at this time only in deacon's orders, and thirty years of age, and he had under him men older than himself, and in priest's orders, a striking evidence of the spirit of the body which was ever ready to cast aside ordinary rules and conventionalities, and to use simply the most effective means to obtain its ends. The other three clerks were all English by birth: Richard of Jutworth, a priest of mature years; Richard of Devonshire, an acolyte; and William of Esseby, a youth

---

[1] The interesting details of the arrival of the Franciscans are now placed within the reach of all by Mr. Brewer's publication of Eccleston's Tract "De Adventu Minorum." In the same volume is contained the valuable collection of Letters of Adam de Marisco, which throw much light on the life of Grosseteste.

still in his novitiate. The five laymen, however, were all foreigners, and, with one exception, Italians. In the first fervour of zeal excited by the new Orders, many men of family and fortune abandoned the world to devote themselves to the work. Placing themselves under the orders of their general, they were ready to accept any post of labour assigned to them, and to leave the sunny lands of the south to work without grudging among the fogs and squalor of our English towns. Conveyed across the channel by the monks of Fescamp, they came to these shores absolutely without resources, dependent upon the charity which they might find. Immediately on their arrival they proceeded to put this charity to the test, and their first experience of it was not very encouraging. They asked entertainment at a nobleman's house near Dover. He locked them up in a strong chamber, and proceeded to take counsel with his neighbours as to how he should treat these strange people. When the brethren, waking from their weary slumbers, tried to depart, they found themselves imprisoned. Being brought before an assembly of magnates, they were accused of being spies and robbers. Then a brother, holding up his cord with a smile, exclaimed, " See ! if we be robbers, here is a cord ready to hang us with." The wise people of Dover then perceived that they must be mistaken in their view of the strangers. At Canterbury they were kindly treated by the Dominicans, who were there before them. They were regaled, not very luxuriously, with ale, so thick that they were obliged to add cold water to make it potable, and the *discus*, or round cake, swimming upon it[2]. Four of the body now proceeded to London, where they established a house on Cornhill, containing cells which were made by stuffing grass between ribs of wood. From London they sent a detachment to Oxford, hiring a house in the parish of St. Ebbe. In both places they were kindly received by the Dominicans, the bitter rivalry which afterwards prevailed between the Orders not having yet sprung up. As yet they had not the privilege of saying Mass, and so were content to remain without chapels attached to their houses. From Oxford they spread themselves to Northampton, Cambridge, and Lincoln. Having thus gained a footing in the country, they began to attract attention, and many came desiring to join the Order. The connexion of Grosseteste

---

[2] "Cakes and ale" was a constant mediæval provision: but probably Shakespeare's "cakes and ale" was of somewhat better quality than that given to the poor friars.

with them as a teacher commenced almost immediately on their arrival at Oxford.   Among them
he found, and at once recognized, congenial minds.
" Many of them," says A. Wood, " had been trained
up in the universities of France and Italy[3]."   What
more beautiful spectacle could be exhibited than
the devotion of pure and cultivated spirits to good
works, even under the most difficult and repulsive
circumstances!   And this spectacle the Franciscans,
in their first establishment, exhibited.   What
wonder if the people of England rushed to do them
honour, if Nicholas de Mulener at once gave for
their use at Oxford a house and piece of ground[4].
The Franciscans applied to Grosseteste to learn the
" subtleties suitable for preaching;" but their great
work was to be done, not alone by preaching, but
chiefly by self-denying labours and ascetic devotion.
They went to the towns, many of which were
scantily provided for by the Church, and most
miserable in their filth and unhealthiness, and here
among leprosy, scurvy, and plague, they laboured
to comfort and instruct the wretched population[5].
They brought a new and vigorous force and life to

[3] " Annals," i. 195.

[4] Brewer, Introd. to " Mon. Franciscan," p. 42.

[5] See the powerful sketch of the work of the friars in Mr.
Brewer's Introduction.

aid the cause of religion, rudely imperilled by the breaking up of society consequent on the Crusades. They were a revival power over all the country, and Grosseteste, who was now to learn to know and love them as their academical teacher, in his after life ever continued to support and cherish them with enthusiastic zeal.

It may seem somewhat inconsistent with the professed great object and design of the friars, with their rules which forbade the possession of books, and others of their characteristics, that they should eagerly have sought a settlement at the chief seat of learning in England, and should have secured as their instructor the most distinguished man of science in the place. But preaching was to be their especial work; through sermons they were to appeal to the neglected and outcast members of the community; and their sermons were not to be mere dry catalogues of the Articles of the Creed, the Deadly Sins, and the Cardinal Virtues, but stirring and earnest practical discourses, put into a popular form, interspersed with anecdote and illustration, calculated to interest as well as to instruct. For help in this they could have applied to no one so well calculated to assist them as Grosseteste. With him theological teaching was not a mere dry repetition of the "Sentences" of Peter Lombard. As he struck out for himself an original path in science, so in divinity also he had the courage to discard glosses and quibbles, and go to the Scriptures, enforcing with clear logic and with copious illustration the weighty truths which he handled. When, therefore, we are told by Thomas of Eccleston that "brother Agnellus, choosing the spot where learning principally flourished in England, and where the great body of scholars was wont to assemble, caused a handsome school to be built on the ground of the brethren, and obtained the consent of Master Robert Grosseteste, of holy memory, to read there to the brethren," we are not surprised to be informed immediately afterwards, that "under him, within a short time, they made wonderful advances both in sermons as well as in the subtle moralities suitable for preaching [6]." Those very "Sayings," from which some extracts are quoted above, may have been delivered as instructions to these zealous and attentive pupils, and we can hardly conceive any teaching more suitable to fit them for their work. It was not long indeed before a revolution was effected in the manner of preaching in England, mainly due, no doubt, to the stimulus given to it by

[6] Eccleston, "De Adventu Minorum," p. 37.

the friars. The old way of *postillizing,* that is, bringing text after text to illustrate a subject, began to be discarded, as did also the other method of delivering a homily or general oration, after the manner of the fathers. It now became the custom to choose a text, and after an introduction of the matter of the subject, to make divisions and application of it. This was utterly distasteful to the older academics, who looked upon preaching as an ingenious rhetorical exercise, and regarded the Scripture text as a sort of cabbalistic words, from which any fanciful meaning might be extracted, without regard to the subject-matter or purpose of the writer. It is impossible not to suppose that the good sense and earnestness of Grosseteste had a great deal to do in effecting this salutary change. A few years later Roger Bacon thus describes the effects of it: " Because the prelates are not much instructed in divinity and preaching while they are in study or conversant in the schools, therefore, after, when they are prelates, and the work of preaching is incumbent upon them, they borrow and beg the boys' exercise-books, who invent an infinite curiosity in preaching by divisions and consonants and vocal concordances, wherein is neither sublimity of speech nor magnitude of wisdom, but an infinite childish foolishness, and a vilifying the Word of God; which curiosity God himself took from the Church, because no profit of preaching could be made by the said way; but the auditors, excited to all curiosity of understanding, even so much that their affections in nothing could be brought to good by those that used such ways in preaching; but although the vulgarity of preachers did use such a way, yet some have another, whereby they do great good, as for example Brother Bertholdus Alemannus, who alone doth more noble profit and good by his preaching than all the brethren almost of both Orders besides[7]."

But though Grosseteste's time and powers must have been severely taxed by his numerous learned writings and his duties as a teacher in divinity, yet besides all this he had other duties to perform at a distance from the University. During the time he was still resident at Oxford he was promoted to no less than four archdeaconries in succession[8], two prebends in Lincoln Cathedral, two livings with cure of souls. In 1214 he was Archdeacon of Wilts, in the diocese of Salisbury, and he ap-

[7] Bacon quoted by A. Wood, "Annals," i. 180.

[8] With regard to the first of these archdeaconries, that of Chester, to which Grosseteste is said to have been promoted in 1213, the authority is very doubtful.

pears to have held this title till 1221, when he succeeded to the Archdeaconry of Northampton, together with the prebend of Erpingham in Lincoln Cathedral. This, again, he exchanged for the archdeaconry of Leicester under the same bishop, and the rectorship of St. Margaret's in that city [9]. Of the eight pieces of preferment which Grosseteste held successively before his final advancement, no less than six were given to him by Hugh de Welles, Bishop of Lincoln. Dr. Pegge, in his "Life of Grosseteste," remarks that he gave him the first piece of preferment which became vacant after his accession to the See, and that there is very good reason to suppose he recommended him for election as his successor to the Canons of Lincoln. Grosseteste speaks of Bishop Hugh affectionately after his death as his "second self," and as having "loved him with peculiar love."

The demands upon Grosseteste's time and labour as archdeacon, rector of a parish, and prebendary of Lincoln Cathedral, must have taken him much away from Oxford during the latter years of his

[9] Luard, Preface, p. 35, who quotes Grosseteste's Roll, still preserved at Lincoln. The other living, to which he was collated in 1225, was Abbotsleigh, in Hunts.

connexion with the University.   He was probably absent from Oxford during the year 1225, at which time he addressed a letter to the Oxford house of Minorites, or Franciscans, to console them for the loss of one of their most distinguished members, Master Adam of Oxford[1], who had gone to preach the Gospel to the Saracens.   But though Grosseteste would, without doubt, labour to the utmost to perform efficiently all his various duties, yet he seems to have discovered that the multiplicity of his work made this almost an impossibility, and we have clear indication that his conscience was troubled about this matter.   " Although, " he says, " it is generally thought that a prebend with a cure of souls attached, and a parish church could be held together, I cannot say I am satisfied in this matter.   On the strength of this opinion I formerly held a prebend of this sort, and a parish church with it, but my conscience pricked me, and I determined to consult the Pope on the point[2]."

[1] Adam of Oxford, is said to have entered the Order on the Feast of the Conversion of St. Paul, 1225, and very soon afterwards to have gone to the Pope, to be employed by him as a missionary to the Saracens.   His death seems to have followed soon after his mission ; but Grosseteste's letter must be put before his death was known to the brethren.   See Brewer's " Monumenta Franciscana," p. 16.

[2] Grosseteste, Ep. p. 242.

This determination to consult the Pope may probably account for Grosseteste's projected journey to Rome at the beginning of the year 1232. He had made all his arrangements for the journey. He was to start about the feast of Epiphany, and he hoped to be back by Whitsuntide. He had obtained the consent of the Chapter of Lincoln, and had arranged that a troublesome claim brought against him by the Convent at Reading, for some arrears of a rent-charge claimed from him as Rector of Abbotsleigh, should be deferred till his return[3]. Suddenly, however, his plans are all changed, and he is obliged to announce to his brethren at Lincoln that he has abandoned the journey. His account of the reasons why he had done so illustrates at the same time the high estimation in which he was held, and the state of affairs between Rome and England at the time :—

"My reason for delaying my journey," he writes to the Dean and Chapter of Lincoln, "is this: being in all readiness for starting, I went to our venerable father, the Lord of Lincoln, whose licence you had been before kind enough to obtain for me, to bid him farewell, as was meet. A discussion took place about my journey, in the presence of my

<hr>

[3] Gross., Ep. iv.

Lord of Bath, the Archdeacons of Lincoln, Northampton, Huntingdon, and Bedford, and many other
discreet and prudent men, who were not a little
anxious, in their love for me, concerning my safety.
In fact they all united in begging my Lord of
Lincoln strictly to prohibit my proposed journey,
and that I should wait to see the event of the
disturbance which had arisen by the plundering
and capture of certain Romans, and as is alleged,
even the murder of some[4]. It was thought that
I should run great danger if I fell into the hands
of the Romans, while, from their recent injuries,
the desire for vengeance was strong upon them. I
determined, therefore, to be guided by this advice,
lest I should rashly incur danger. I trust the
Lord will not impute to me this delay, and that
you will not ascribe it to levity and inconstancy[5]."
It is evident from the tone of this letter that
Grosseteste felt very strongly on this subject of the
journey to Rome, and if we are right in inferring
from the passage quoted above that his strong feeling in the matter arose from his uneasiness about

[4] These were the disturbances which originated under the
leadership of Sir Roger de Twenge, a full account of which will be
found in Chapter XII.

[5] Gross., Ep. iii.

his preferments, we can the better account for the two following events in history. These are detailed in a letter to his sister Juetta, which will sufficiently explain itself. "You desire to know the state of my health, and are eagerly anxious that I should communicate it to you in a letter. Suffice it to say that before the Feast of All Saints, I was seized with a severe attack of fever, but by the divine blessing I recovered, and am now restored to my former health. You know, too, that I have resigned all the income[6] which I had, except the prebend which I hold in the Church of Lincoln. You, as a religious, and vowed to observe a rule, cannot be vexed if of my own will I become poorer in money, that I may be made richer in virtues—if I despise the world to gain honour with the citizens of heaven—if on account of the good of obedience I have abandoned temporal things, seeing that there is no way to heavenly things save by obedience. The good which you cherish in yourself, that ought you more earnestly to cherish in

---

[6] *Reditus omnes.* He may have still retained his archdeaconry, as there was probably no *reditus* from that, but only the payment of fees. It was the *parochiales ecclesiæ*, two or more of which he held, about which he was so anxious. Probably at this time also he resigned the Chancellorship of Oxford, if he had held it up to this.

me in proportion as we are nearer by the ties of blood. True religion renounces the world, according to the word of truth, which says, ' Whosoever forsaketh not all that he hath cannot be My disciple.' As you, therefore, who have made profession of religion, love in yourself these and such like good things of religion, do not grudge to me some attempt at good things, though it be a weak one; be content that I have laid aside the heavier part of the burden which weighed me down; yes, rejoice greatly that I am freed from that which, were I not free from it, would destroy me[7]." It is rather a matter of wonder that Grosseteste with these views and in this state of religious enthusiasm, which was coincident with the weakness produced by the attack of fever, did not altogether abandon the world, and cast in his lot with those Franciscan friars whom he so much loved[8]. For the sacrifices which he made, however,

[7] Gross., Ep. viii. Juetta, the sister of Grosseteste, was probably a nun at Godstow, or some religious house at or near Oxford. When Grosseteste is bishop, Adam Marsh writes to him from Oxford about her, mentioning first her illness, and in a subsequent letter her death, and asking whether Masses should be said for her. (Mon. Franc., 95, 164.) It would seem from the tone of this letter that the poor nun took pleasure in her famous brother's career, and was vexed at his resigning his preferments.

[8] Matthew Paris distinctly says that such was Grosseteste's intention, p. 722.

he appears to have been severely taken to task by his friends. They objected to him the folly of throwing away revenues which were justly his own, and they also objected to him that it was altogether wrong to withdraw from the pastoral care, and having once put his hand to the plough to look back. To these criticisms he answers in a letter addressed to Adam Marsh, his dear friend, a Franciscan friar, who had succeeded him as instructor to the settlement at Oxford. He thanks him cordially for his sympathy and approval in the matter of his resignation, and as regards the charge of foolish sacrifice, he repeats what he had said to his sister as to the dangers and drawbacks of the goods of this world. "I know," he writes, "by experience, and still am I suffering from it, how many thorns there are in riches, how great occasions of sin, how seldom they are well spent, how often they make their possessor not richer, but poorer." With regard to abandoning the pastoral office, he says: "I was pressed by my utter inability of performing as I ought those duties which with too little circumspection, and with too great boldness I had undertaken, and I was also pressed by the obedience which I owed to the Apostolic See." He concludes his letter very touchingly: "In fine,

my dear friend, I beseech you with tears, cease not
to pray God for me, that if what I have done be
ill, He would pardon it of His infinite mercy with
my other sins great and innumerable; but if it be
good, as I the rather hope, that He would of His
mercy cleanse away the blemishes which circumstances may have wrought in this and any other
good thing that I may have done ." That Grosseteste was penetrated with an intense and absorbing
religious sentiment there can be no doubt. His
resignation, whether a mistake in judgment or not,
is a practical proof of this, and it is further evidenced
by a letter written about this time to some clerk
who had been living licentiously, and who is
described as one that had been long his friend, and
as older than himself, though at this time Grosseteste was approaching his 60th year. The letter,
like all Grosseteste's, shows a masculine power and
vigour, and could not, we should imagine, have
failed in making an impression. " You," he begins,
" whom formerly I was accustomed to love in
Christ, I cannot but continue to love for Christ, for
' Charity never faileth;' but, I say, I cannot love
you now in Christ, but for Christ; for, as fame
with loud and noisy tongue declares, you are not

<hr>

[9] Gross. Ep. ix.

in Christ,—for from the body of Christ you are separated by the deceitful and filthy disease of licentiousness, which joins you to the body of the ancient enemy,—the name of Christ through you is blasphemed, the holy Scripture through you is held in abomination, inasmuch as you set it forth with the mouth of a body which is abominably polluted. You are a stain on the clergy, a disgrace to theologians, and the joy of the enemies of the truth. You are a scorn, a song and a tale, to the whole people. Return, I beseech you, to yourself. Remember your body, which is weak, poor in appearance, wasted by disease and age, bald, wrinkled, near to the grave. Remember your profession, that holy order to which the vow of chastity is joined, that cure of souls which needs the example of chastity. Remember that you are a teacher of the Holy Scriptures, a preacher of the Cross of Christ, and how inconsistent with these duties is your disgraceful licence. Add to these things, the fear of hell, and the love of the blessedness of heavenly joys, and by all these arguments brought together extinguish that foul eagerness for loose living which possesses you[1]." The earnestness of this appeal declares the spirit of the writer.

[1] Gross. Ep. x.

Possessed by an overwhelming sense of the great and solemn nature of his office, Grosseteste desired rather to withdraw from it than to fill it imperfectly; but when called into the front of the battle, where he felt that he could do a good work for his Master, he allowed no love of learned ease, no timid shrinking from responsibility to stand between him and his duty.

CHAPTER IV.

GROSSETESTE AS REFORMER.

1235—1237.

Grosseteste made Bishop of Lincoln — His letter about the place of his consecration—The See and Cathedral of Lincoln—Grosseteste's severe reproof of one who presented for a living an illiterate deacon—His deep sense of the responsibilities of his office—His anxiety to have friars as his assistants—He determines to hold a visitation of his diocese on a new plan — His letter to his archdeacons — The abuse of letting churches in farm — The establishment of vicarages — The secular employments of the clergy—The exemption of the clergy from the secular law—Great task undertaken by the bishop.

For somewhat more than two years (1232—1235) Grosseteste remained without holding any special office in the Church or the University. His sole preferment was a prebend in Lincoln Cathedral. An order issued by King Henry III. in 1234, bearing on the discipline of Oxford, mentions the Chancellor, Master Robert Grosseteste, and Friar Robert Bacon, as three persons specially designed to assist in carrying it out. This is conclusive evidence that Grosseteste was not at that time Chancellor, and it is probable that he had ceased to hold that office for a considerable period. During this interval, with his mind in its ripe vigour, and his time free from distractions, Grosseteste may have produced many of those numerous and valuable works, which even now remain in such vast profusion. But the Church was not long to continue deprived of his great abilities, earnestness, and zeal. On the 7th or 8th Feb, 1235[1], died Hugh de Welles, Bishop of Lincoln, the constant friend and patron of Grosseteste, and a man of a kindred spirit with his. He is described by one monkish historian as "the foe of all religious men[2]," and by another as "The persecutor of monks, the crusher of canons and all religious persons[3]." These expressions probably imply nothing more than that he made some attempt at enforcing

---

[1] It should be remembered that the year of that era commenced with the Feast of the Annunciation; so that the date of Bishop Hugh's death would appear in Chronicles as 1234.

[2] Roger de Wendover.

[3] Matthew Paris.

discipline in the numerous religious houses of his
vast diocese. That he was popular with his own
Canons of Lincoln is probable from their immediate
election of his close ally and firm friend—one who
had been his most distinguished archdeacon and
representative—to be his successor. Grosseteste
had indeed been long a member of the Chapter
of Lincoln. His fame had become as it were
identified with Lincoln; but he was a person of
low birth, he had lately shown by his resignation
of his preferments somewhat of the ascetic spirit,
and the canons must have known pretty accurately
before their election what manner of man he was.
They themselves had probably retained much of
the same characteristics which had distinguished
the body on the election of St. Hugh. We are
there told that in their state and revenues the chief
Canons of Lincoln were equal to bishops, and when
Henry II. sent for them and bade them elect the
poor Burgundian monk, they received the order
" with derisive laughter [4]." On this occasion, however, they do not seem to have received any order
specially as to the person whom they were to

[4] See "Magna Vita St. Hugonis" (Ed. Dimock).   At St.
Hugh's death the canons claimed a right of free election.   See
Hoveden.

choose. The Congé d'eslire appears to have left
them free[5], thus recognizing the first enactment of
Magna Charta; and on 27th March, 1235,
Robert Grosseteste was elected Bishop of Lincoln
by the Dean and Chapter. On April 5 the king
approved the election, and sent his letter to Archbishop Edmund Rich to confirm it. On April 16,
the temporalities were restored, and in June he
was consecrated at Reading, along with Hugh,
Bishop of St. Asaph[6]. The particular day of his
consecration it is not easy to ascertain. It varies
from May 18 with some authorities, to September
29 with others. The day for which there seems,
most authority and likehood is June 17[7]. The
particular place of his consecration—the Abbey

[5] As to the election and confirmation of bishops things were in
a great state of confusion at this time. Magna Charta had
specially conferred upon the clergy the right of free election, but
this, though granted in theory, was constantly overruled by the
King or the Pope forcing their nominees on the Chapter, or refusing to confirm those who had been elected. There were, however, some apparently free elections about this time, and, amongst
others, this of Grosseteste appears to have been so. See Collier,
B. v. The Congé d'Eslire was issued Feb. 19.

[6] Pegge's "Grosseteste," p. 35, note.

[7] This is the day of the martyrdom of St. Alban, and may
probably have been selected for that reason. The consecrating
bishops were Edmund, Archbishop of Canterbury; Jocceline,
Bishop of Bath and Wells; Robert, Bishop of Sarum; Hugh,
Bishop of Ely; and Ralph, Bishop of Hereford. (Pegge.)

Church of Reading—was an unusual one, and the monks of Canterbury protested against it, claiming as a right that all the suffragans of the Province of Canterbury should be consecrated in the metropolitical church. Archbishop Edmund, who had himself been consecrated only the year before, was at the time on bad terms with the monks of his cathedral, and not inclined to gratify them by bringing within their reach the fees and offerings which would accrue from the consecration of a bishop in their church. A curious and interesting letter from Grosseteste to the archbishop on this subject is worth quoting, as it illustrates the state of mind in which the former came to his high office: "The Apostle, writing to the Romans, says, 'Judge this rather, that no man put a stumbling-block or an occasion to fall in his brother's way,' and presently after he adds, 'If thy brother be grieved with thy meat, now walkest thou not charitably. Destroy not him with thy meat for whom Christ died[8].' It is plain that in nothing which is indifferent ought we to give offence to a brother. As then, as I truly believe, the monks of Canterbury will not be prevailed upon to agree with good

[8] Rom. xiv. 13, 15.

will that I should be consecrated any where except in the church of Canterbury, and as, if against their will I am consecrated elsewhere, they, being offended at this matter, in itself indifferent, will fall into the pit of anger, rancour, and hatred, and appealing against your action will set on troubles and expensive suits; and as 'the servant of God ought not to strive,' and 'it is utterly a fault if Christians go to law with one another,' 'lest we should offend them,' destroying 'some weak one for whom Christ died, and not walking charitably;' inasmuch as consecration may be given to me without any offence or scandal at Canterbury, I most earnestly beseech your holiness to consent to consecrate me in the church of Canterbury for it is better to be consecrated there, *however great the expense may be,* than elsewhere with any amount of saving, if the weak brother be offended, for whom Christ died, inasmuch as the word of truth testifies, 'Woe to that man by whom the offence cometh[9].'"

In spite, however, of this earnest and solemn appeal to the archbishop the consecration took place at Reading. The monks of Canterbury agreed at last to withdraw their opposition

[9] Matt. xviii. 7. Gross. Ep. xiii.

under protest that the fact was not to be drawn into a precedent[1]. It was some time before the final ceremony of the elevation to the episcopate—the enthronization in the cathedral church—was performed, and during the seven months which intervened between his consecration and his first visit to Lincoln, much was done by the new bishop in his important work. The diocese of Lincoln at that time contained the Archdeaconries of Lincoln, Leicester, Stow, Buckingham, Huntingdon, Northampton, Oxford, and Bedford, and extended from the Humber to the Thames. The dioceses of Lichfield and Worcester bounded it to the west, and those of Norwich and Ely to the east. The cathedral of the northern part of this diocese had originally been at Lindisse, Sidnacester, or Stow, but in the troubled period of Danish invasions the original diocese had become amalgamated with that of Dorchester. Hence its huge bulk and vast extent. Remigius, the first bishop of the Norman race, had brought back the chief seat of the diocese to its first locality, and the Saxon Church of St. Mary, on the hill of Lincoln, had been rebuilt and beautified by him. He abandoned his original title of Bishop of Dorchester and assumed

<hr>

[1] Pegge, p. 36.

that of Bishop of Lindisse[2]. The original church of Remigius had lately been replaced by a fabric of surpassing beauty, due to the skill, taste, and munificence of the Burgundian monk of the Grande Chartreuse, the justly celebrated St. Hugh of Lincoln. In this magnificent edifice, with which he had long been connected as prebendary and archdeacon, Grosseteste was enthroned, and there he now lies buried. Even before his consecration, while yet only bishop elect, the new prelate had clearly shown of what spirit he was, and on what principles he meant to administer the great trust committed to him. A monk had brought to him for institution to a benefice a certain deacon who was dressed in bright-coloured clothes, adorned with rings, and altogether of the exterior of a foppish layman. When the bishop elect proceeded to question him, he found him quite illiterate. Upon this his anger broke forth against the monk who had presented him. " You !" he exclaimed, " a monk! making profession of perfection with your religious habit and vow, and bound by these

[2] It seems that there was a good reason why Remigius did not take the title of Bishop of Lincoln. There was at the time of his consecration a Bishop of Lincoln in existence, a suffragan of Dorchester. Stark's " History of the Bishoprick of Lincoln," pp. 475, 89,

to mortify the carnal life for the salvation of souls! —with what face do you dare to present for the cure of souls one who, by bearing and habit, evidently shows himself rather the slayer than the healer of souls? Our Lord Jesus Christ gave His precious blood, yea His very life, to a most bitter and shameful death, to save and quicken each individual soul; and do you strive to hand over so great a number of souls to one who by his bad example will betray and destroy those souls, for each of which Christ gave his whole life? The sheep which you buy for twelve pence you would not give up to the wolf, and the soul which Christ bought with His precious blood, which is a price incomparably greater than the whole creation, you endeavour to hand over to the destroyer! Is it not the fact that the sheep valued at twelve pence is more valuable in your eyes than the soul valued at the blood of Christ? You, who thus dishonour Christ and his precious blood, are you not manifestly on your way to perdition?" Appalled by this solemn language, the monk and his nominee departed, and went to their friends to complain of this severe treatment, whereupon the bishop was subjected to a railing and bitter letter on the subject. His reply is couched in the language of the purest Christian charity. He willingly accepts rebuke, but at the same time he shows the perfect justice of what he had said and done, and suggests that if his censors were true lovers of Jesus Christ, they would not blame him, but join with him in his censure of those who had sought thus to degrade the pastoral office[3]. The same overpowering sense of the importance of the pastoral charge breathes in another letter written by Grosseteste at the very commencement of his episcopate. Eager to find capable and learned men to assist him in his labours, he had summoned William de Cerda, a reader or professor in the University of Paris, to some important charge in his diocese. The invitation had not been altogether rejected by the scholar, but he had excused himself for the present inasmuch as he was occupied with his theological course at Paris, and was unwilling to take preferment, the duties of which he could not fully discharge. To combat this resolution, Grosseteste writes to him, commending his zeal for study and his sense of the importance of the pastoral care, but very earnestly remonstrating with him as to his preference of the less important over the more important: "The Lord says, 'If thou lovest Me, feed My sheep,' but

[3] Gross. Ep. xi.

He nowhere says, 'If thou lovest Me, read in the professor's chair to the shepherds of My sheep.' . . . I supplicate you with my whole heart's devotion, I entreat you by the sprinkling of the blood of Jesus Christ, that you would not refuse to take upon you that cure of souls to which you are drawn, not by me only, but by Christ who gave for them —all and each of them—the whole price of His blood. Truly Christ and the whole community of heaven is drawing you by the bands of love, is driving and urging you by the terror of the punishment of hell, which He threatens fearfully to those by whom the pastoral care is obstinately refused when they are called to it[4]." Animated by the same intense seriousness of purpose as regards the efficient performance of the pastoral office, the new bishop writes to Brother Alardus, the Provincial of the Friars-Preachers in England, begging him to allow him the help of John de St. Giles and Geoffrey de Clive for a year. The former Dominican, we learn by a subsequent letter addressed by Grosseteste to himself[5], was exercising his gifts as a preacher in a foreign land, and Grosseteste appeals to him with great force on the claims that

[4] Gross. Ep. xiii.   [5] Ep xvi.

his own native soil had upon him. " You are indeed
a debtor to preach the word of salvation to all, but
especially to those who by the band of nationality
are bound to you as brethren. Therefore the
Apostle, as you know, specially wishes himself ' to
be accursed from Christ for his brethren, his kinsmen
according to the flesh[6],' that is to say, the Israelites.
I am persuaded that there is no spot where your
presence is so urgently needed as by me and your
dear friends who are with me ; nor is there any
bishop who so much requires your help in preaching the word of salvation as I do, burdened as I am,
beyond all others that I know, with this mighty load
of the pastoral care[7]." It may probably be inferred
from the mention of the " dear friends who were
with him," that Geoffrey de St. Clive had already
joined the bishop. He desired to have these
two Dominicans to be assistant-preachers who
might be constantly with him, especially in that
general visitation of his diocese which he was
already contemplating. They were to " support
him when weak and wavering, to be props and
stays to him when slipping and likely to fall, to
encourage him when he feared, to stir him up when

[6] Rom. ix. 3. [7] Gross. Ep. xiv.

F

he hesitated, to be the censors and directors of him and his people[8]."

In the same spirit, and to the same purport, he wrote soon after to one more famous than either of those above mentioned, his dear and intimate friend and former pupil Adam de Marisco, or Marsh, who subsequently reached so high an eminence of fame as the "illustrious doctor" of the Franciscans. Adam had written to him some advice for which Grosseteste thanks him most heartily, declaring, "you alone have I found to be a true friend, a faithful counsellor, one who regards truth not vanity, one who reposes on a solid and firm support, not on an empty and frail reed."

In other letters the same earnest desire to have the friars with him, to help him in his episcopal work, is repeated and enforced. Writing to Helias, the Minister-General of the Franciscans in England, he speaks of his brethren as being more specially near to him in the bands of love, and inasmuch as his diocese is "much wider than any other in England, much more populous," he presses earnestly upon him his request that, if possible, he may have four Franciscans assigned to him, to help him in "the preaching of the Word, the hearing of con-

[8] Gross. Ep. xiv.

fessions, the appointing penances," in all which he held them to be the most valuable assistants he could have, and the most helpful supplements to his own deficiencies[9].

It must be evident to all, that the bishop, in so earnestly desiring to have a staff of friars to assist him, was animated by no other motive than earnest zeal to benefit the souls of his flock. The help which the devotion and skill of the early friars offered, was the readiest to his hand, and was at once grasped at by him. Whether, however, he showed a solid judgment in thus vigorously patronizing this irregular ministry may be fairly open to question. The friars, confident in the support of Rome, soon began to overset the influence, and cripple the work of the parish-priest. They would intrude into a parish (as Matthew Paris tells us), and with their wooden altar, on which they fixed a little consecrated super-altar of metal, would proceed at once to say Mass, and then, assembling the people, they would promise them easier and lighter penances if they confessed to them[1]. This would naturally exasperate the parish-priest, and against such an intrusion as this he ought to have had a

<hr>

[9] Gross. Ep. xli.
[1] MatthPariew s, " Hist. Major," p. 419.   (Ed. 1640.)

remedy by applying to his bishop.   But Grosseteste had thrown himself entirely on the friars' side, and it would not seem as though any complaint against them would be likely to find much acceptance with him.   On the contrary, he directs his archdeacons to "compel the parish-priests to make their people listen attentively to the sermons of the friars, and humbly to confess to them[2]," and writing to a neighbouring prelate, Alexander de Stavensby, Bishop of Lichfield, he speaks with somewhat of a severe tone on the opposition which he had ventured to offer to the establishment of the friars at Chester[3].   But though in his zealous patronage of the friars Grosseteste may have been wanting in far-sighted policy, yet for his present need there seemed to be no more suitable helpers.   The state of the diocese may very fairly be judged by the questions of inquiry issued by his predecessor, some five years before the end of his incumbency[4].   The first of these questions is, "Are any rectors of churches, or vicars, or parish-priests, scandalously illiterate?" Other questions follow which denote a great absence of reverence in sacred things, and a

----

[2] Gross. Ep. cvii.   [3] Gross. Ep. xxxiv.

[4] Printed in Wilkins' "Concil.," vol. i., from a very ancient MS.   These are probably the most ancient Articles of Inquiry which exist.

loose state of morality in the clergy met by a very
inefficient and almost nominal discipline.   The
bishop, who had been one of the archdeacons who
had carried out these articles of inquiry, knew
doubtless exactly the state of things with which
he had to contend.   Hence his desire to have
a staff of active workers to assist him in the
visitation which he designed at once to carry out
with uncompromising vigour.   The idea of a personal visitation made by a bishop throughout his
diocese, was altogether a new one.   The notion
of the day was, that the bishop should be a sort of
temporal prince occupied in high matters of State,
and, ecclesiastically, a judge of the last appeal;
that the discipline of the diocese should be worked
by the archdeacons, under whom were to be employed the rural deans, called in the satires of that
day, "the archdeacon's dogs," and under them
again the *bedelli*, or sompnours[5].   But this method

[5] "The Deane is th' Archdeacon's dogge that can the foote find out,
　　And by the scent can seek where he may lucre gett,
　And can by sleight bring in clerkes purses all about,
　　Whom he had caught before within his master's nett."
Mapes' Poems, Old Trans.

　The sompnour in " Chaucer " will be remembered, who,
　　" If he found owhere a good felawe,
　　　He wolde techen him to have non awe
　　'In swiche a case of the archdecknes's curse."
Prologue to " Cant. Tales."

of administering a diocese by no means satisfied Grosseteste's views of the episcopal responsibilities. He himself describes what he calls his "new and unaccustomed proceedings." "I, as soon as I was made bishop, considered myself to be the overseer and pastor of souls, and therefore I held it necessary, lest the blood of the sheep should be required at my hand in the strict Judgment, to visit the sheep committed to me with diligence, as the Scripture orders and commands. Wherefore, at the commencement of my episcopate, I began to go round through the several archdeaconries, and in the archdeaconries through the several rural deaneries, causing the clergy of each deanery to be called together on a certain day and place, and the people to be warned, that, in the same day and place, they should be present with the children to be confirmed, and in order to hear the word of God and to confess. When clergy and people were assembled, I myself was accustomed to preach the word of God to the clergy, and some friar, either Preacher or Minorite, to the people; at the same time four friars were employed in hearing confessions and enjoining penances; and, when the children had been confirmed, on that and the following day, I and my clerks gave our attention to in-

quiries, corrections and reformations, such as belong
to the office of inquiry.   In my first circuit of this
sort, some came to me to find fault with these
proceedings, saying, 'My lord, you are doing a new
and unaccustomed thing.'   To whom I answered,
'Every new thing which instructs and advances a
man is a blessed new thing;' nor could I suppose
at that time, that on account of this my visitation,
any mischief would afterwards fall on those placed
under me[6]."   Having determined upon holding
this personal and thorough visitation of his diocese,
the bishop,—either as a preliminary proceeding to
guide them in the inquiries which they were to
bring before him, or during his visitation, to
animadvert upon those abuses which he found most
rampant,—addressed a letter to his archdeacons,
which has been preserved to us.   He begins by
alluding to the words of the Epistle to the Hebrews,
that ministers must watch as those who have to
give account for the souls of their flocks[7], and bids
them, in some matters, persuade and teach their
ignorant flocks, and in others use stronger measures.   The first great abuse against which they
were to contend was that of drinking; and with

[6] Wharton, "Anglia Sacra," ii. 347.
[7] Heb. xiii. 17.

this view they were strictly to prohibit the *Scot-ales*, which seem to have been very prevalent at that time, and of which sometimes notice was given in the church itself [8]. To these drinking-matches the clergy were much addicted, as we gather from various inquiries and constitutions, and they also seem to have encouraged and assisted in certain rough and boisterous games in which wooden rams were raised upon wheels, and opposing parties charged each other to contend for the mastery. Against all games, on festival days, Grosseteste would have his archdeacons warn clergy and people, quoting St. Augustine to the effect that the women had better spin, and the men plough,

[8] This appears in the "Constitutions of St. Edmund." "We forbid notice of Scot-ales to be given by the priest." The *Scot-ales* (Scotalli) appear in all the ecclesiastical documents of the period, as well as in the popular verses. They are described by Archbishop Edmund as a "revelry in which the drinkers bind themselves by mutual agreement to drink off each the same amount; and in which he is considered to be the champion who makes all the rest drunk, and is able to bear the greatest number of cups without being overcome." (Wilkins' "Concil. Const. Ep. Edm.) The "ale," or the "nale," as it was written in the thirteenth century, is often alluded to in poems—*e. g.* Robert de Brune (1303)—

> "At plays and festys, and at the nale,
>   Men love to lesten trotevale:"

—*i. e.* love to listen to scandalous and loose stories.—See also "Complaint of the Ploughman."

than thus profane holy seasons.   A caution against the scandals arising at vigils is given, and we also hear of the funeral feasts being turned into loose and riotous orgies, and of plays and interludes celebrated in the church and churchyard[9]. But perhaps, still more curious is it to have grave directions against mothers and nurses overlaying their infants in bed[1].   The archdeacons are also warned to prohibit private marriages, and to set their faces steadily against parish processions, in

[9] It is sometimes supposed that in the darker ages (called occasionally " the ages of faith ") veneration and respect for holy things was especially prevalent.   The very reverse, however, was the case.   Veneration for holy things was almost unknown, as the following facts may serve to show:—(1.) The Eucharist was carried through the streets without any reverence.   (2.) When the priest celebrated, the laity were accustomed to throng into the chancel and press round him.   (3.) The *super-altars*—pieces of stone or metal, fixed in the wood of the main altar—were often taken out and used for grinding and crushing colours. (4.) The chrism-cloths which had been wrapped round the baptized child were used for secular purposes.   (5.) Plays, profane as well as sacred, were constantly exhibited in the church. (6.) Law-suits were commonly pleaded in churches.   For all these, and abundance of other, forms of sacrilege, see William de Wadingtoun's poem, " Manuel des Pechiez " (not much after Grosseteste's time), and the English expansion of it by Robert de Brune (1303).   Also, " The Constitutions of Alexander de Stavensby " (Wilkins), " The Enquiries of Hugh de Welles " (ditto), " Constitutions of Archbishop Edmund " (ditto), and Grosseteste's " Constitutions."

[1] This appears in all the Constitutions of the period.

which, on the occasion of the annual visitation of the archdeacon, rival parishes, with their banners, used to contend with one another for precedence, and blood was often shed in the senseless strife. The avaricious and simoniacal spirit of the clergy, is to be carefully repressed, inasmuch as they were wont to exact the Easter offering before they admitted their parishioners to Mass, and to refuse the other sacraments, except on the payment of a fee. One especial point to which Grosseteste paid attention in his visitation was the state of the revenues of the churches. The revenues of the livings were at this time very generally grossly misapplied. The practice was, when a benefice was obtained, for the rector to let it out "to farm;" that is, to contract with some third party, usually a monastic body, to give him so much annually for the revenues of the parish, and to get the church work in it done at as cheap a rate as possible. It is evident that this was an utter misappropriation of church funds, and a scandalous abuse; but it was greatly encouraged by the monasteries, who, having many priests in their body, could contract for the performance of any amount of parochial services, and by their powerful organization were able to compel the payment of tithes. Accordingly all monastic annals contain frequent records of their receiving churches "in farm."

The holding of preferment by those who did not perform the duty was permitted and encouraged by Rome, as the Roman incumbents absorbed in the earlier part of the thirteenth century a great part of the Church revenues of England. It was convenient for them to make a compact with some religious house to farm their benefices, often, doubtless, at a small part of their real value, but which they might securely enjoy at a distance without any trouble taken for it[2]. Early in Grosseteste's episcopate he was called upon to express his opinion about farming churches. The gross abuse of the Roman intrusion into English benefices came before him in this shape, and he was called upon to act in the matter. In what way he would act could not be a matter of hesitation with Grosseteste, though, from his extreme deference to Rome, he speaks more mildly in the matter than he otherwise

---

[2] Thus we have in the "Annals of Dunstable:" "We presented to the Church of Sheppingley a certain Roman—to wit, Peter Vitelli—to whom we contracted to pay ten marks yearly." "Dunstable Annals, Ann. Monast." iii. 176. This was evidently a way to reconcile the monastic houses to accepting the Papal Provisions, as they would have the opportunity of making something substantial out of the churches assigned to foreigners.

would. He thus writes to John, the Roman, Subdean of York: " We have received the letters of the venerable Lord Boethius, Nuncio and intimate of the Pope, asking, on your behalf, that we should allow you freely to dispose of your church of Chalgrave. Not only you, but also all rectors of churches in our diocese can freely dispose of their churches; indeed, we shall compel them to do so. Surely, however, your wisdom must perceive that putting a church to farm is not freely disposing of it, but rather reducing the free faith of Jesus Christ to a servile condition. . Nor can we see that on your part there can be any good reason for putting your church to farm. The necessity of residing elsewhere does not prevent your having a prudent and faithful deputy, and religious bodies are not to be considered as answering the description of 'an honest person in orders,' as the Council (Oxford) directs. Moreover, religious bodies ought to preach contempt of the world in all their works, but by their ' farmings ' they preach the exact contrary, to the great danger of religion, and the loss of many souls. If, therefore, I should allow such a farm, I should clearly be a disobeyer of the Council of Oxford. I should be betraying also the souls for whose salvation I am pledged to labour, and for which I am even to be ready to die. . . . I am prepared to do any thing out of affection for you, which I may do without offence; but, though you are my friend, yet is the truth of God a still closer friend, as you yourself would desire, who, indeed, love truth more than yourself."   In this religious spirit did the bishop prepare to grapple with this great abuse.   But the evil custom of pluralities and non-residence upheld by Rome for the double purpose of enriching its useful instruments, and making gain for itself by granting dispensations; and the greed and cunning of the "religious" houses, proved too strong to be easily overthrown.   The bishop had, in many cases, to yield or accept a compromise.   Of the first we have an instance in the Annals of Dunstable. "This year," says the chronicler, "Robert, Bishop of Lincoln, held a general visitation of his diocese.   In each archdeaconry he held General Chapters, and preached and published his Constitutions.   He suspended many rectors of churches; some he allowed to clear themselves; from others he took bonds binding them to forfeit rank and benefice if they should fail to observe continency hereafter.   And at that time we had great difficulty in obtaining from the bishop the churches which we held at farm for three years[3]." In the midst of the confusion and disorder which prevailed, the bishop had been constrained to yield this point, but evidently not without a severe struggle to rectify the abuse. Of the way of meeting the evil by a compromise, the Annals of Tewkesbury Abbey furnish us an example. It is recorded there that the lord abbot went to Bishop Grosseteste, to consult him about the church of Great Marlow, "how it best might be converted to the use of the monastery." Scarcely could the abbot have asked a question more likely to irritate the man to whom he applied. We are not surprised to hear that he "met with a severe rebuff." Finding that the bishop would not sanction appropriation, he then proposed appointing a youth of a noble house (Gilbert de Clare), who, of course, on institution, would have been ready to let the church in farm to the abbey. This, too, Grosseteste refused, but he suggested, as a way of compromise, that the abbey should appoint a fitting priest, and that it should reserve out of the revenues of the benefice an annual pension[4] to be paid to Gilbert de Clare, until such time as he should be provided with another benefice[5]. To

<hr>

[3] "Annal. Monast.," iii. 147.
[4] Twenty-six marks,—a considerable sum in that day.
[5] "Annal. Monast.," i. 122.

this compromise, which he no doubt felt to be unsatisfactory, but which seemed the only way of avoiding the scandal of farming, Grosseteste was obliged to have resort on several other occasions.

Closely connected with the question of farming was that of the establishment of vicarages[6].

The *appropriations* of churches which were so eagerly sought by the monasteries were in fact the perpetual establishment of all the evils of farming. There was no one responsible person to whom the cure of souls was entrusted. The religious house undertook to provide the needful ministrations, but evidently there was no security for their performance, and no way by which the bishop could enforce it. Hence, very soon after appropriations of parish churches to monasteries began, a canon framed by Archbishop Anselm was passed in the Council of Westminster, " That monks do not accept churches without the bishop's consent; nor so rob of their revenues those that are given them, that the priests who serve them be in want of necessaries." This canon, however, did not check the acquisition of churches by the monasteries. The

<hr>

6 Dr. Pegge thinks there were none before the Norman Conquest. See his able disquisition on Vicarages, Appendix vii. to " Life of Grosseteste."

bishop's consent, or the Pope's dispensation, was procured; patrons of livings were induced, for the good of their souls, to make over their advowsons to monasteries; and, not very long after the enactment of the canon of 1102, the parishes possessed by the monasteries amounted to more than one-third of all the livings of England [7]. Even nunneries, which could not undertake to supply ministers, possessed many appropriate rectories. The abuse having got to this head, the only remedy was to force the religious houses to devote some portion of the tithes, or land of the livings, to endow permanently a priest, who should in all respects, except his pay, stand in the place of rector of the parish. This was ordered by the Lateran Council in 1179, and soon afterwards the first traces of the establishment of *vicarages* in England begin to appear. The " religious" houses opposed the arrangement with all their influence, but the bishops gradually succeeded in founding vicarages, though, as they were often imposed upon by the appropriators as to the value of the benefice, the payments which they ordered were not invariably fair to the vicar. Bishop Hugh de Welles, Grosseteste's predecessor at Lincoln, esta-

[7] Pegge, Appendix vii. They were computed at 3845, when all the livings of England amounted to 9284.

blished many hundred vicarages, as his Roll still remains to testify.   In the Dunstable Annals we have a record of his proceedings as regards that priory [8].

It would appear that about five marks was held a fair payment for a vicar [9], but there is no doubt that this payment, as well as the appointment of vicars altogether, was constantly evaded by the religious houses.   Wherever this was found to be

[8] "The same year, in October, vicarages were constituted, and set at a fixed sum, in the churches which the Canons of Dunstable have for their own use, a careful inquisition having first been made of the value of the churches and of the vicarages, and it having been considered which churches were the best able to maintain vicars.   The appointments were entered in the bishop's register in this manner: 'The vicarage of the Church of Hod-ham ought to consist of the whole altar-dues of the church and Vivian's croft, of about seven acres, reserving to the prior out of the said altar-dues one mark and the tithes of the lambs.   The value of the vicarage is estimated at six marks, and that of the whole church at twenty.   The whole church of Totternhoe is worth twelve marks, but the vicarage five.   This consists in the whole altar-dues of the said church, and the rent of tenpence from the land of Richard Godwer, and the parsonage-house, and the half of a tenth of hay from the whole parish. . . The vicarage of Husborn Crawley is worth five marks and four shil-lings, and consists in the whole altar-dues and a parsonage-house, with a croft and a meadow on the south side.   The whole church is worth twelve marks: and be it known that the prior has to sustain the burden of receiving the archdeacon when he visits, and has to keep up the books, the chancel, the vestments, the vessels, and tallage."

[9] 3*l*. 6*s*. 8*d*.

the case, he instituted and appointed a vicarage.
Next, after the establishment of vicarages, the
point of ecclesiastical discipline which seemed to
Bishop Grosseteste most pressing, was to prohibit
any secular employments of the clergy on any pretence whatever.   In his view bishops could not for
a moment be justified in performing judicial duties
or executing offices of State, nor could abbots or
clerks of any rank be allowed to act as justices
itinerant, or in any subordinate lay function. When
we contrast these views with the opinions and practice of the bishop's day[1], and of many centuries
after it, Grosseteste will indeed appear to be a man
before his time. To William de Raleigh, Treasurer
of Exeter, the bishop writes: "As regards, indeed,
the interests of the realm, I don't see that any mischief can arise by your stay in Court, but as regards
your own soul it is full of the greatest peril, and
therefore as I am anxious for your salvation, with a
father's love, it is hurtful to me.   You have a
large pastoral care which has a claim upon you for
more labour than you can give, even if you were
altogether free from secular business[2]."   Writing

[1] "The judges of the King's Courts had until the reign of
Henry III. been principally ecclesiastics." Hallam, "Middle
Ages," ii. 22.
[2] Ep. xxiv.

to Archbishop Edmund he says, " According to the
canons it is not permitted to any clerk to exercise
secular jurisdiction under any prince or secular person, and if any clerk offends against this he ought
to be exiled from the ecclesiastical functions, and
regulars, if they attempt it, should be more severely
punished [3]."   He therefore calls upon the archbishop to inhibit an abbot from acting upon the
king's commission, and to assist him in stopping
this abuse.

Connected with this question of the performance
of secular duties by ecclesiastics, there arose the
much more important question of the relative
authority of the civil and ecclesiastical powers.
What would be the result if the archbishop, as
Grosseteste desired him, should stop a clerk from
performing the commission assigned to him by the
king's writ? Whatever the result might be, Grosseteste in his great zeal was prepared utterly to
disregard it. " It is better," he says, " to endure the
most bitter and disgraceful death, even an infinite
number of times, than to sin even once." In his
view the ecclesiastical was far above the secular
authority. Thomas Becket never put forth more
extreme views on this point than the Bishop

[3] Ep. xxvii.

of Lincoln. Thus he writes to William de Raleigh : " Let no one deceive himself in thinking that secular princes can appoint any thing and cause it to be observed as a law, which opposes a divine law or a *Constitution of the Church*, without separating themselves from the unity of Christ's body, the Church, and incurring everlasting doom to the fire of hell, as well as the just overthrow of their authority.   For secular princes, whatever power they have ordained by God, and whatever dignity, receive these from the Church ; but the princes of the Church receive no ecclesiastical power or dignity from any secular power, but immediately from the ordinance of God, nor can he who receives rebel against him from whom he receives it, by means of that which he receives.   Secular princes ought to know that both swords, the material and the spiritual, are the swords of Peter.   The spiritual sword is used by the princes of the Church, who occupy the place of Peter, by themselves ; the material sword is used by the princes of the Church by the hand and ministry of secular princes, who are bound to draw the sword which they carry at the orders of the ecclesiastical princes, and again to put it up as they direct.   In the same way, both ecclesiastical and civil peace, and both ecclesiastical and civil law, are committed to those who hold the place of Peter; but temporal peace, and temporal law, Peter and his vicars administer by the agency of secular princes; whereas spiritual peace and spiritual law, they administer themselves. . . . . Therefore, the laws of princes must yield to the divine laws, and not oppose the laws of the Church; and if, either by act of violence or by enactment of law, a secular prince opposes Christ or the Church, he is to be considered disobedient to Christ who begat him with the word of truth [4]."

In judging the bishop on this matter we must not take our views from the state of things existing in modern days, when the laws of the State are exactly settled and scrupulously administered. In his time the State was constantly committing acts of encroachment and injustice; the law of the land was doubtful and obscure, while the canon law lately made into a complete system, was universally held to have the first claim on the obedience of all churchmen. It is curious that the two points which Grosseteste so earnestly pressed —the non-employment of ecclesiastics in judicial functions, and the freedom of clergymen from pro-

[4] Ep. xxiii.

ceedings in the temporal courts—mutually defeated one another. "Now," says Mr. Hallam, writing of this period, "abstaining from the exercise of temporal jurisdiction, in obedience to the strict injunctions of their canons, the clergy gave place to common lawyers, professors of a system very discordant from their own. These soon began to assert the supremacy of their jurisdiction by issuing writs of prohibition whenever the ecclesiastical tribunals passed the boundary which approved use had established. They succeeded also partially in preventing the impunity of crimes perpetrated by clerks[5]."

It will be seen by what has been said, that the bishop had set himself no slight work to perform in undertaking the visitation and correction of his vast diocese. Evils and abuses had grown up to a great head in the Church. On every side there was ignorance, negligence, contempt for law, perversion of endowments. All these evils Grosseteste determined to meet, and by God's help, to overcome. But we have as yet only touched upon matters connected with the parochial clergy, or as they were usually called, *the seculars*. The class of evils and abuses due to the monasteries was

<hr>

[5] Hallam, "Middle Ages," ii. 22.

even more difficult to deal with. But before we touch on these it will be necessary to say something of a General Synod of the English Church which took place at this time at London, and of the part which Grosseteste took therein.

CHAPTER V.

GROSSETESTE AS REFORMER.

1238—1244.

Growth of the power of the Pope's Legates in England —Grosseteste readily welcomes the Cardinal Otho— His unbounded deference for the Papal officers— Goes to the Council of London—The Pope's policy in not allowing Churchmen to hold lay offices and pluralities—Protest of Walter de Cantilupe— The Legate yields—The Canons of the Council of London—published by Bishop Grosseteste in his Constitutions—Complaints against the severity of his visitation—Attempt to poison him—His vigourous measures to correct the Monasteries—Origin of the quarrel between the bishop and the Chapter of Lincoln—Progress of the dispute—The chapter invoke the king's authority—Grosseteste deprives the dean and appoints a new one—Bad effect of the quarrel upon the bishop—The chapter resorts to a gross forgery—The bishop and the dean prepare to go to the Pope at Lyons.

THE unhappy reign of John had handed over England as an actual fief to the Court of Rome, and the Pope, Honorius, had deliberately undertaken to govern this land, not as a Judge of Appeal, but as a ruler of the first instance, controlling and legislating in all matters. In order to carry out this astounding usurpation it was necessary for Rome to be represented by a viceroy, who, while paying a nominal deference to the native rulers, should in effect control every thing both in Church and State. This was the foundation of the power and authority of Legate, which grew to such astonishing proportions in the earlier part of the reign of Henry III. The first Legate of this reign was Gualo,—"a feeble, avaricious man, who seems to have plundered without shame, and intrigued without success[1]." He was succeeded by Pandulph, a man of consummate skill and art[2], who taking advantage of the political weakness of the country, its threatening foes without, and the ill-blood between king and barons within, managed to direct every thing as he pleased, and to reign as practical sovereign of the country. At length, however, the good but somewhat timid regent, Hubert de Burgh, combining with the Primate, Stephen

---

[1] Shirley's Preface to " Royal Letters," p. xix.

[2] Pandulph had played a conspicuous part in the transactions between John and the Pope, and knew the country well.

Langton—a man of a noble English heart—the power of Pandulph was broken; and the archbishop even obtained a promise from the Pope that, so long as he (the archbishop) lived, no resident Legate should again be appointed to England. For a time it would seem that the English party had obtained the ascendancy; but the king's foreign connexions and companions continually excited him against the English. An evil counsellor was found in the person of Peter des Roches, Bishop of Winchester, and the king entered into a conspiracy against his people by dismissing his English counsellors, and inviting over 2000 mercenaries, to whom the custody of the royal castles was to be entrusted. Against this danger Archbishop Edmund Rich with his suffragans made a noble stand. They threatened the king with excommunication if he did not break off his evil designs, dismiss Peter des Roches, put away his foreign favourites, and rescue England from a base subjection to a foreign power. "The kingdom" they say indignantly, "has been made a tributary, and this land, the queen of provinces, has (oh, shame!) been, like to those of no repute, placed under tribute[3]." The king knowing that the

[3] Matt. Paris, p. 396.

bishops had the barons at their back, was obliged
to yield, and Archbishop Edmund, who at the time
of this remonstrance was not yet consecrated, thus
proved himself a noble successor of Stephen Langton. As soon as it was really ascertained that the
new archbishop was firmly devoted to the national
party, the treacherous king and his evil counsellors
determined to supersede his authority by again
procuring a Legate from Rome. Against this
Archbishop Edmund remonstrated, and all patriotic hearts in England revolted. " But the king
despising the advice of his counsellers refused to
change his resolve. The Legate therefore came
with pomp and great power. Famous bishops and
clerks ran to meet him to the shore ; some went in
boats to meet him with cheers, and carrying the
most valuable presents. Yes, some bishops sent
messengers to Paris to meet him, and to offer him
scarlet fabrics and precious vessels. The king went
to the shore to greet his arrival, and bowing his
head to his knees, conducted him into his kingdom
with the greatest observance; and the bishops,
abbots, and parsons received him with all honour
and reverence, with processions and ringing of
bells and precious gifts, as much as was fitting,

aye, and far more than was fitting[4]." Was Bishop Grosseteste one of those who thus eagerly pressed forward to welcome this foreign cardinal who came to help the king to conspire against the liberties of his subjects? We know not, but it is clear at any rate that he accepted and acknowledged the Legate, and took no stand against his pretensions. We have a remarkable letter written by Grosseteste to the cardinal soon after his arrival, when, with the intrusive audacity of the representative of the Pope, he had appointed one of his clerks to a prebend in Lincoln Cathedral without consulting the bishop. Grosseteste informs him that he had given away the preferment before his nomination reached him, and argues that it is objectionable to give away preferments without the consent of the patron, especially when that consent might so easily be obtained. At the same time he professes the most unbounded devotion to the Roman See. "God knows," he says, "that if the Pope or you ordered it, I would go to the utmost regions of the Saracens at your bidding. I know, and truly know, that my lord the Pope and the holy Roman Church has this power, that it can order as it pleases

<hr>

[4] Matt. Paris, p. 440.

concerning all ecclesiastical benefices." "Your holiness's wisdom ought not, by giving this prebend without consulting me, to have put to confusion my littleness which is most devoted and most obedient to you, especially as I was always ready, and am still ready, as far as that prebend goes, and further still, to provide for any of your people; not under compulsion, so as to bring confusion on myself and my church, but of my own will and to promote love and charity between us, although since my consecration a nephew of my lord the Pope has been promoted to one of the best prebends of the Church of Lincoln. I humbly beseech your holiness, therefore, to recall the collation to the said prebend, lest I, the most miserable of men, should not be able to lift up my face to you, or else not to my brother bishops and those over whom I am placed [5]." Nor is this the only instance in which Grosseteste expresses unbounded deference and devotion to the intermeddling and usurping Legate. Not long, probably, after the date of the letter quoted above, the same cardinal wrote to him, desiring him to institute the nephew of Earl Ferrars to a benefice, although he was but a boy and not in holy orders ! What does the bishop, with his intensely strong views of pas-

<hr>

[5] Gross. Ep. xlix.

toral responsibility reply to this audacious mandate? " God knows I desire to carry out the requests and commands of your fatherhood most promptly and most obediently; I trust also that you will not ask for, or command any thing which troubles my conscience. But, as you well know, the wiser and bolder are not troubled, when often the more timid conscience is troubled, and the more perfect man can do that which the less perfect cannot safely undertake. I am in that state of imperfection as to have a timid conscience, especially in the matter of the pastoral charge, and this will not allow me to institute the said Thomas, as he now is, to the pastoral care. . . I earnestly, therefore, entreat your holiness to persuade the said lord to present some suitable clerk to the said church, or else as your holiness can do many things lawfully which my imperfection cannot do save unlawfully, *I hand over to you all that appertains to me in this matter of the admission of the said Thomas to the said church,* firmly hoping that you will order in such a way as will be profitable for souls." Then follow suggestions as to a clerical substitute being provided if the young unordained boy be instituted[6]. Would, indeed, that this letter did not exist among the epistles

6 Gross. Ep. li.

of Grosseteste, but when we put it side by side
with the epistle in which he justifies his indignant rejection of a deacon because he had not the
tonsure and wore smart clothes, we are compelled to
recognize with somewhat of shame the extent to
which a blind devotion to Rome led even so highly
principled a bishop as Grosseteste. But here, at
any rate, we get a foundation for understanding
how much the final indignant protest, which Roman
oppressions wrung from the bishop, signified.
" Grosseteste's behaviour in this matter," says
Dr. Pegge, " must be resolved into that blind and
indiscriminate submission, which at this period of
his life he conceived was due to the commands,
how erroneous soever such commands might be, of
the papal omnipotence [7]." It was in this spirit of
entire devotion to the cause of the Legate that
the Bishop of Lincoln proceeded to break off for
a time his visitatorial work and to meet Cardinal
Otho at the council held in London on the morrow
of the octave of St. Martin (November 19), in the
year 1237. A violent opposition had been stirred
up both among clergy and laity to the legate's
proceedings. He was obliged to be guarded by a
large band of mercenaries, and when he entered

[7] Pegge's Grosseteste, p. 79.

St. Paul's on the cold November day, as Matthew Paris describes it for us, he did so with fear and trembling when he saw the unfriendly looks of those around him.   He had come to the council prepared to carry out a scheme of fine Roman policy—a scheme which, having the appearance of devout care for the highest interests of the Church and of religion, was in reality designed to do nothing less than to put the nomination to all the chief offices of the State into the hands of the Pope.   The plan was, that the Council of London should adopt and promulgate the canons of the Council of Lateran, lately held, one of which was that no ecclesiastic should hold any secular employment without a dispensation from the Pope.   Now, as in reality there were but few laymen fitted for high and difficult employments, this was simply giving to the Pope, through his dispensation, the appointments to all State offices[s].   Ardent and devout churchmen, as Grosseteste, were to be reconciled to this by its apparent entire scrupulous conformity to canonical law; but men who not only cared for canons, but who had also at heart the best interests of the State,

---

[s] See Dr. Hook's able remarks on this subject, and his excellent account of the Council of London. "Lives of the Archbishops," vol. iii. c. iii.

scrupled to support it, and on this subject Archbishop Edmund, and Bishop Grosseteste, both of
them men of the highest character, were opposed
to each other[9]. We have seen the eager and
earnest manner in which Grosseteste set himself to
oppose the secular employment of the clergy, how
he was himself ready to withstand the king's authority on this point, and how earnestly he exhorted
Archbishop Edmund to take the lead in these prohibitions. But while we give Grosseteste all credit
for zeal, we attribute greater insight and keener
judgment to the archbishop. To make Papal dispensations requisite for every thing, was indeed an
obvious method at the same time of replenishing
the exchequer, and of extending the power of the
Pope. And this, there can be no doubt, rather
than a zeal for enacting canons of church discipline,
was the real reason for assembling the Council of
London. It was supposed that the canons of the
Lateran Council would be received without opposition. It was calculated probably that there would
be no churchman of weight, who, whatever his
practice might be, would be found bold enough to

---

[9] Dr. Pegge speaks very slightingly and unfairly of Archbishop
Edmund, who showed himself a much wiser man in this matter
than Grosseteste.

stand up in the council and defend, as a matter
of principle, the holding of pluralities or the secular employment of clerks.   But the Legate and his
party miscalculated in every thing.   Their designs
were at once penetrated; the barons gave an unhesitating support to the clergy in resisting them;
and a bold and blunt-spoken prelate, Walter de
Cantilupe, Bishop of Worcester, was found to stand
up and warn the Legate that he had better not
meddle with pluralities,—that the old who had lived
in honour all their life, and kept good hospitality,
did not want to have to change their ways now, and
that the young, being fiery and impetuous, might
be excited to violence by any such interference. As
for his dispensations, he said they did not want
any of them[1].   Although the Bishop of Worcester
spoke from an entirely worldly point of view, yet
his words seem to have fallen in exactly with the
spirit of the assembly.   In fact every one knew
perfectly well (with the exception perhaps of Bishop
Grosseteste, and a few unworldly devout men like
him) that the proposed prohibitions did not proceed
from a love of ecclesiastical discipline, but from a
desire to multiply dispensations.   The Legate, trembling before the strong show of opposition, at once

[1] Matt. Paris, p. 448.

withdrew the proposed canons by referring the bishops to Rome, and the critical part of the business being settled, the more formal part went smoothly forward. A large body of canons was enacted for the English Church, which were indeed little more than a repetition of the Constitutions of Archbishop Edmund, published the year before[2], and which, like most mediæval canons, were somewhat more for show than for use; the laxity of most of the bishops, and the irregularity and ignorance of the clergy being too strongly developed to be healed by canons. To no one perhaps in that council were the canons adopted by it so deeply interesting as to Bishop Grosseteste. He was in the midst of the arduous struggle against the abuses which these canons assailed. He had himself been questioning and investigating, rebuking, reproving, and punishing the evils which they condemned. Full of zeal for the episcopal work he was determined to the utmost of man's ability to carry out genuine discipline, and as far as man's ability went, he did so. Shortly after the conclusion of the Council of London he put forth, for the use of his diocese, his *Constitutions,*—a long and elaborate code of laws and directions, at the same

[2] Dr. Hook, "Lives of the Archbishops," iii. 198.

time embodying the canons of London, and specially illustrating the state of ecclesiastical matters in the diocese of Lincoln.

The labours of his diocesan visitation were now renewed by the bishop with as great zeal as ever, and, as might be expected, the severity with which he prosecuted his inquisition, his readiness to use the full extent of his authority without scruple when he had discovered an abuse, stirred up vigorous opposition against him. We find from a letter of his to Archbishop Edmund, that numerous appeals had been made from the diocesan to the metropolitical authority. The Abbey of Oseney which had been sequestered by him, complains that on this ground they cannot pay the fifty marks, for which they farmed the Church of Iver, belonging to Boetius the " Pope's friend." Grosseteste replies that this is a mere shuffle, as the fifty marks were due for the time before their rents were sequestered. Hugh de Ravel complains that the bishop had unfairly kept him out of his living at Woodford. Grosseteste replies that he is too youthful to be admitted to a living, and indirectly complains of the archbishop having appointed a commission at Cambridge in the matter, which had summoned him before it. The Arch-

deacon of Bucks and Walter de St. Quentin complain against Grosseteste's unfair treatment of
them in their suit against John de Crakhall, one
of his friends. The bishop replies that he had not
acted as judge in the suit, but had referred it to
commissioners. But, says he, "inasmuch as the
pastoral care claims my entire devotion, and far
more than I can give for the salvation of souls, I
humbly beseech you that I may not be troubled
by such frivolous appeals, which by suppressing
truth and suggesting falsehood, try to evade the
ordinary jurisdiction of prelates, and thus be taken
away from attending to those things which are of
God to mind those things which are of the world,
or rather those things which are of discord. I
beseech you that your prudence may provide
against such annoyances as these, and find wholesome remedies for them, and that the divine
wisdom which is in you may detect these snares of
worldly subtlety, and put to flight the darkness of
fraud, and make plain the way to those who wish
to direct their feet into the way of peace and
eternal salvation[3]." The unprincipled men who
were met and thwarted by the energy and upright
zeal of the bishop were, however, ready to go even

[3] Gross. Ep. xxvi.

to greater lengths than appeals to the metropolitan, and, accordingly, we are hardly surprised to hear that this bold champion who ventured to interfere with the claims of the monks to pillage the Church for their own aggrandisement, was assailed by poison, sometime during the year 1237, and that, according to the historian, he was " with great difficulty brought back from the very gates of death[4]." His cure the bishop owed to one of those friars whom he so much loved, and whose proficiency in medical studies now stood him in good stead.   It was John de St. Giles, of whom we have before found Grosseteste speaking in terms of affection, who successfully treated him.   We learn this from a notice by Matthew Paris of an attempt to poison the Earl of Gloucester some years afterwards, when it is said that the same skilful leech was the means of restoring him to health, as had formerly restored from a like malady Robert, Bishop of Lincoln[5].   Very soon after his consecration, Grosseteste removed from their places no less than seven abbots and four priors.   These were the Abbots of Leicester, Owston, Thornton, Nutley, Bourne, Dorchester, and Messenden, and the Priors of St. Frydeswide, Coldnorton, Bradwell, and De la

----

[4] Matthew Paris, p. 440.   [5] Matt. Paris, p. 974.

Lande[6]. So vigorous an attack proclaimed at once the spirit in which the bishop meant to deal with the monasteries. He was determined to act towards them according to their own rules, and to judge them according to their own laws. He did not admit that privileges or pretences of any sort should exempt men who had vowed themselves to "religion" from really endeavouring to promote that which they professed to promote, or excuse them from the most plain and fundamental requirements of the moral law. It was not as a foe to asceticism and the monastic life as it stood in theory, that Grosseteste was so severe upon the monks, but as a stern reformer, recalling men to obligations which they had utterly forgotten and ignored. Doubtless the attempts made by these men, negligent of their own rule, to invalidate the episcopal authority by obtaining exemptions, and to interfere with the efficiency of the parochial clergy by getting advowsons and farming benefices, increased his anger against them. Still, had not the monastic system of his day been thoroughly steeped in negligence and corruption, it would hardly have been possible even for one who stood so high in public esteem as Grosseteste, to have made so terrible a raid upon the

6 Ann. Dunstab. Ann. Monast., i. 143.

Benedictine abbots without a general outcry being raised against him. None such, however, appears to have been raised, and we even have intimations that his severity was not considered sufficiently thorough.

Adam de Marisco writes to him that he much regrets that some suggestions made by foolish persons had prevented Grosseteste doing, while he was at Banbury, in the matter of Godstowe Abbey and certain other religious houses, what he had earnestly recommended him to do. What this was may be inferred from the fact that Flandrina de Brewes, Abbess of Godstowe, was afterwards deposed by the bishop, and Adam de Marisco again writes to him that the visitation which he had made at Godstowe had been most salutary[7]. Of the three Oxford religious houses, none had escaped his castigation. St. Frydeswide's had seen its prior deposed, Oseney its revenues sequestrated, and Godstowe its abbess removed, and had been otherwise visited. On all sides it was perceived that there had succeeded to the episcopal throne a man of unaccustomed energy and courage, a prelate willing to spare no abuse however highly placed, and guarded by old prescriptions; a prelate who

7 Monumenta Franciscana, pp. 99, 107, 117.

did not fear even to stretch his authority to the uttermost to reduce what he felt to be crying scandals. It was only natural that those who had long enjoyed immunities and exemptions, who had been left to govern themselves, and to exercise power over others without accounting to any superior, should take fright at this new and invading influence, and strive with might and main to turn aside its course from themselves. Such, doubtless, were the motives which prompted the Dean and Chapter of Lincoln,—a great, a rich, and a powerful corporation,—to set up their claim for exemption both for themselves and for their affiliated churches, from the bishop's jurisdiction. The claim thus set up only excited the bishop to overthrow the exemption demanded at any price. His labour, care, and money were expended without stint or scruple to bring this about. In his letters, he seems to represent the issue of the strife as one of vital importance to the Church, and as it was a new and unsettled point, the whole of the Church of England looked on with anxious interest as the strife proceeded. The bishop felt that if a large number of churches was to be withdrawn from his inspection by their connexion with the cathedral, a barrier would at once be placed in his way against

an effectual and remedial visitation. He claimed
then to visit the prebends, *i. e.* the churches
attached to stalls in the cathedral, in the same way
as other churches. But the chapter stoutly opposed this. They had always exercised an exempt
jurisdiction. They had their court and their judge,
called Dean of Christianity[8], who decided on all
disciplinary matters for the parishes belonging to
the cathedral, and whose decisions were liable to
be reviewed by the dean as chief ordinary, but in
no way to come before the bishop. Grosseteste,
by way of meeting the difficulty boldly, claimed not
only to visit the churches attached to the cathedral
but the chapter itself. This was an unheard-of
thing. Matthew Paris relates it with amazement
and indignation, as though it were a terrible inno-
vation. "The Bishop of Lincoln proved himself
the bruiser[9] and savage persecutor of the religious
in his diocese. He even rose up against the canons
of his cathedral church, who had elected him, and
insisted that, putting aside the Dean of Lincoln,
they should submit to be visited by the bishop
himself against the custom of that church

[8] We find the same office existing at Evesham (see Annales de
Evesham), and at Exeter. The title is still retained as that of a
rural dean.

[9] The mallet (malleus).

for time out of mind[1]." As soon as he had found his claim to visit resisted by the chapter, the bishop had first tried the effect of conciliatory and explanatory letters[2], in which he sets forth, on grounds of reason and Scripture, the justice of his claim. The canons, however, were deaf to arguments of this sort. They had determined from the first to carry the matter to the Pope, where they believed, according to the custom of that court, the claimants of exemption would be sure to find a favourable hearing. Almost immediately on the commencement of the dispute they had despatched a proctor to the Papal court, knowing that the bishop had already an agent there. In the meantime the bishop, who declares himself most anxious to end the suit satisfactorily to all concerned, submitted certain proposals for its settlement to the dean and chapter. The first proposal was to refer the whole matter to the Legate, Cardinal Otho. The second was to refer it at once to the Pope. Both these proposals were rejected. Why the second was rejected does not seem clear, inasmuch as the chapter had from the first calculated on going to the Pope, and had despatched their proctor

---

[1] Matt. Paris, p. 485.
[2] Gross. Epist. lxxi. lxxiii.

to his court. The third proposal which they accepted was that they should obtain from the Pope the appointment of certain commissioners to judge of the dispute in the first instance, naming as the commissioners to be employed, the Bishop of Worcester (Walter de Cantilupe) and the Archdeacons of Worcester and Sudbury, and that, if they could not decide the matter, it should be referred to the Pope, all action being in the meantime suspended. This provision is held by Matthew Paris to have much compromised the rights of the canons. "For," he says, "the bishop never had visited, and he cannot be said to cease who never had begun, as Diogenes cannot be said to lose the horns which he never had. On the other hand, the dean, for whom the canons contended, would cease to visit, and thus would appear to be deprived of that which he possessed, even if he ceased only for an hour; on which account complaints were multiplied, and a very grave scandal began to arise[3]." The canons had no sooner made the agreement to refer than they began to repent of it, probably on the ground indicated by Matthew Paris. Abundance of suggestions and remonstrances would no doubt have been addressed to them by the other chapters of England, whose interests

[3] Matt. Paris, p. 485.

were felt to be at stake, and they were perhaps severely taken to task for having compromised the cause. They seem to have shown their annoyance and vexation by some fresh insubordination to the bishop, not allowing him to enter the chapter-house [4]; "and," says Matthew Paris, "it repented them bitterly that they had placed such a bishop over themselves, a man of such low extraction, and this they protested publicly in the presence of the bishop [5]." Grosseteste, on the contrary, though considering the arrangement of referring to arbitrators a concession on his part, yet had no wish to disturb the arrangement, and wrote to the Pope and to Cardinal Otho to effectuate it [6]. As, however, the chapter was anxious to break through it, it did in fact soon come to nothing. Matthew Paris says, "After a great deal of quarrelling, and a considerable expense uselessly incurred on either side, the matter was carried to the personal decision of our lord the Pope [7]."

The cause was thus fairly landed in the great appeal court of the Pope, and each party prepared for the strife. Odo of Kilkenny was the agent for the chapter; the bishop was represented by

<hr>

[4] Matt. Paris, l. c.   [5] Matt. Paris, l. c.
[6] Gross. Ep. lxxxi. lxxxii.   [7] Matt. Paris, p. 485.

Simon de Arderne. It is evident that, though the canons stood well on the general issue, as seeking an exemption against a diocesan bishop, yet their case was somewhat prejudiced by the fact that Grosseteste had been armed with the Pope's authority when first he attempted the visitation, and hence they stood in the position of those who were resisting the Pope. Although the quarrel was now referred to the Pope for final adjudication, it still continued to rage in England. It would seem that Grosseteste's character was one that would not really allow of any compromise. He might consent to refer a cause to the Pope, but being never for a moment doubtful as to his own rights, he could not help acting as though the decision were already in his favour. Thus, he did not cease to press his visitatorial claim, although the matter was under the judge. The chapter, on their side, determined to leave no stone unturned to gain their object, had procured from the king a prohibition inhibiting the bishop's judges from proceeding in any matter between himself and the chapter. By thus venturing to call in the secular arm against the ecclesiastical they had, as the bishop reminds them, incurred the sentence of excommunication, for, according to the Oxford council, "those are excommunicated who maliciously endeavour to break through or disturb the liberties of the Church[8]." But Grosseteste did not confine himself to remonstrances and expostulatory letters. Satisfied that great unfairness and underhand dealings had been shown by the chapter, he proceeded to inflict censure upon their head and representative. He first suspended the dean, William de Tournay, and then, as this probably was disregarded, he deposed him, and, by an arbitrary stretch of his authority, appointed as his successor his own most intimate friend Roger de Wescham. Roger de Wescham had been previously made by the bishop Archdeacon of Oxford, and he was one in whom he could thoroughly trust; but by what arguments he could persuade himself that it was just or fair to advance him to the deanery of Lincoln, it being the undoubted right of the canons to elect their dean, seems hard to understand. The reception which the new dean met with from the canons was, as might be expected, a very discourteous one. They excommunicated him at once, and the bishop replied to this by excommunicating their proctor Nicholas. This was a sad and miserable state of things, and it did not fail to cause great

<hr>

[8] Gross. Epist. xcii.

pain and scandal to good men, friends of the
bishop. Thus his dear friend Adam Marsh writes
to expostulate with him, and to exhort him to
strive rather to be loved than feared, and the Dean
and Chapter of Salisbury also write to him to plead
for peace. The bishop replied that peace was most
desirable, and that the only thing that hindered it
was the obstinate refusal of the chapter to yield the
points in dispute. "You ask and beg me to be ready
to make peace between the chapter and myself.
You should know that peace is that which above
all things I ardently desire. But the sort of peace
which I wish for is the peace of order, in which in
all quietude the inferior parts yield to the superior,
the equal parts do not grudge their equality to
those equal to them; and the superior parts grant
the influence of their kindness to the inferior, without diminishing in any way their own authority.
To such a peace as this, which is the gift of Him
'who is our peace, who hath made both one,' I
shall ever be inclined, and I cannot suppose that
men of your discretion ask me to consent to any
other sort of peace; for any other sort of peace
would rather be the disturbing of true order, a
mere apparent quieting, but a real confusing[9]."

[9] Gross. Epist. xciii.

But although expressing himself anxious for peace, the bishop, about the same time, wrote very angrily to the chapter, and threatened them with excommunication.

The quarrel in which he was thus engaged brought out, on the bishop's part, symptoms of a harsh and overbearing temper; but on the side of the chapter even far worse qualities were developed. Matthew Paris says somewhat strangely, that the canons were so worried and persecuted by the bishop, that they were compelled to divulge and exhibit a certain paper to avert from them the yoke of this new slavery. And what was the paper thus doubtfully introduced? It purported to be an authentic document which recorded the fact of the foundation of the see of Lincoln as a new see in the time of William Rufus, the ancient see of Dorchester having altogether lapsed and ceased to exist, and there having been a long interval between its complete extinction and the foundation of the new bishopric of Lincoln. The document further declared that under the authority of two cardinal legates, eight archbishops, and sixteen bishops, a solemn settlement was made for the government of the secular canons who composed the chapter. This provided that the dean should

have power to administer discipline and to suspend
the canons, if necessary, and that only if his discipline failed, he might call in the bishop, and
after him the king[1].   It is hardly necessary to say
that this document was a complete forgery, falsifying the facts of history, and bearing its own refuta-
tion on the face of it.   It would be somewhat hard
to discover in England in the time of William
Rufus, *two* cardinal legates and eight archbishops.
The forgery was a clumsy one; but the object of
it was at the same time to throw out the bishop
from the right of visitation, in the first instance,
and also to enlist the king in the matter.   But
Grosseteste was determined that with him there
was but one place where an authoritative decision
could be obtained—a place to which as yet he felt
unbounded devotion and entire reverence.   To the
Pope's court the bishop determined personally to
proceed, and the dean, as representing the chapter,
was prepared to meet him there.

[1] Matt. Paris, p. 571.

CHAPTER VI.

GROSSETESTE AS REFORMER.

1238—1244.

Grosseteste's high ideal of the monastic state—Contrast to it in the state of the monasteries in his diocese—The Priory of Minting—His harshness towards monks accounted for—His anger with the Monks of Hertford—His quarrel with the Abbot of Bardney—The Monks of Canterbury excommunicate him—His indignation at this—His extreme assertion of episcopal rights—His views as to lay patronage—His plain speaking to the king as to the way in which he ought to treat the Church—He successfully withstands the king's attempt to extort money.

In order to preserve the continuity of the dispute with the Chapter of Lincoln, many important events in the bishop's life have for the moment been omitted. We now recur to the time when, after the Council of London and the publication of his Constitutions, Grosseteste was still busily occupied in his great work of meeting and removing the abuses which seemed to assail him on every side. The monasteries were his great difficulty. We have already seen how in the commencement of his episcopate he was compelled to depose no less than eleven heads of religious houses. The contrast of that which he actually found existing in his diocese, with his own ideal of what a monastery should be, must have been a continual trial to him. What his ideal was may be gathered by a letter sent by him to the Convent of Peterborough, in which he translates for the monks from a Greek original some high sentiments on the monastic state. "These things," he concludes, "I have been careful to lay before you, as a silver mirror, that you may behold therein the form of monastic life. And if the excellence of the holiness of monastic life be so great, who does not perceive how discordant it is if the place where the monks are kept, that is the monastery, be not sanctified? Who is there, who, if he were about to entertain an earthly prince, would not cleanse his house, adorn and deck it in every way, with all his strength and resources? Who would wish to spare toil or expense, until the habitation were prepared as well as possible with all decoration? But in your monastery the King of Heaven continually dwells, not alone by His divine attributes, but also in the sacrament of the Eucharist by the true substance of flesh which He took of the Virgin. The greatest beauty of the corporal tabernacle is the glory of the holiness which it receives in its dedication to Him[1]." But with this high ideal the state of many of the religious houses around him painfully jarred. Especially was he tormented with the state of the Priory of Minting, a daughter-house of the foreign Abbey of Fleury, where the grossest irregularities seem to have prevailed. He writes to the Abbot of Fleury: " You send to us from your monastery, to the Cell of Minting in our diocese, men who live licentiously with harlots; men who have separate funds of their own[2]; disobedient, given up to debauchery, drunkenness and amusements, and who are not ashamed to eat flesh even four days a week. Therefore, although your way of life in your own house be according to the rule which you have professed, yet in this, which I have mentioned, there is a base and notable stain upon you. I have expelled from the aforesaid house one Philip for fornication, possessing property, disobedience, vagabondage, eating flesh against the rule,

<hr>

[1] Gross. Epist. lvii.   [2] Proprietarii, v. Ducange, s. v.

of all which offences he has been judicially convicted. I have expelled also Theobald and Walrond,
and Gerard, for being in like manner possessors of
property, intolerably disobedient, wanderers about
the country, frequenters of disreputable houses,
addicted to unlawful sports, even more than seculars, and, in a word, such open and enormous transgressors against the observance of their rule as to
be the scandal and the song of the whole country [3]."
With such cases as these to deal with, it is not to be
wondered at that the bishop was stern and severe.
In fact, sternness and severity were what he himself professed and desired to have imputed to him.
Writing to the Abbot of Leicester, who had found fault
with him on this ground, he says, " You suggest to
me that I have a heart of iron and one lacking
pity. Would that, indeed, I had this heart as hard
as iron,—a heart that could in nowise be softened
by the blandishments of seducers,—a heart so strong
that it could not be broken by the terror of evil-
doers,—a heart so sharp that it would cut in pieces
all vices and dislodge all opposing evils. Of that
hardness which the prophet Ezekiel had, would that
even a small share might be granted to me by Him
who is the true Rock, concerning which the Apostle

[3] Gross. Epist. cviii.

peaks, 'That rock was Christ[4].' If, indeed, I am hard as iron in cruelty and obstinate malice, pray ye the Lord for me, that He would be pleased to take away this hardness and grant me His gentleness; but if I am hard as iron after the manner of the prophet, pray ye the Lord that this hardness may ever, as long as I live, receive an increase[5]."

It is very observable that Matthew Paris, from whom all the accounts of Grosseteste's severe dealings with monasteries are drawn, does not, on account of these highly coloured statements, pass an altogether unfavourable judgment on Grosseteste for justice and equity. Speaking of the miracles which are said to have happened at the bishop's tomb, he says, "And let no one be inclined to doubt these on account of certain hasty actions which are written in this volume as having been done by him in his lifetime. Truly, Robert was wont to thunder terribly against the monks, and still more terribly against the nuns. Confidently, however, do I assert that his virtues were pleasing to God, although his excesses displeased Him. It was with him as with David and Peter[6]." "It is sufficiently clear," says Dr. Pegge, "that the

<hr>

[4] 1 Cor. x. 4. [5] Gross. Epist. iv.
[6] Matt. Paris, p. 880.

bishop was not the enemy of the monks when they followed the rule of their respective Orders, and that he ought not to be taxed with injustice and oppression for endeavouring to correct their vices and irregularities [7]." These remarks may serve to qualify the accounts of some violent outbreaks of temper which have to be related of the bishop in connexion with monasteries. One of the most striking of these was the way in which he dealt with the town of Hertford. Intending to visit that town, Grosseteste had sent before directions to the abbot and monks to be ready to receive him. They, not over eager to have so dangerous a guest, declined the honour. On this the bishop, excessively indignant, proceeded to put under an interdict the whole town, including the secular churches. So strange and incongruous a sentence at once brought the matter before the Legate, and the bishop was induced or obliged to withdraw his interdict [8]. Soon after this the bishop presented himself at Dunstable to hold a visitation.

The house of Austin canons, at Dunstable, was one deeply tainted with the bad aggressive spirit which prevailed so extensively in the monasteries, as its own Annals sufficiently show. The canons

---

[7] " Life of Grosseteste," p. 141.　　[8] Matt. Paris, p. 879.

trembled at the coming of so vigorous a corrector of abuses. He insisted that each of them should take an oath to purge himself from complicity in any abuses. One of them, Walter de Gledelle, rather than face this ordeal, fled from the monastery and professed himself a monk at Woburn Abbey[9]. But the monastic quarrel which made most noise in the country, and in which the bishop seems to have acted as arbitrarily as in any case, was that of Bardney. The rich and famous Benedictine house of Bardney had acquired a special historical interest from having shared, with Croyland and Peterborough, the terrible cruelties of the Danes in Anglo-Saxon times. Its monks were murdered, its buildings ruined, and for many years it lay entirely waste; until, after the Norman Conquest, Gilbert of Gaunt, the nephew of the Conqueror, bethought him of restoring the desolated sanctuary and endowing it with divers goodly manors for the good of his soul. His pious design was further carried out by his son Walter; the Bishop of Lincoln and King Henry I. concurred and assisted, and the king granted to Bardney the same privileges as appertained to royal abbeys of his own foundation[1]. This great religious house situated

<hr>

[9] Ann. Duns., iii. 152.   [1] Dugdale, Monasticon, i. 683.

only ten miles from Grosseteste's cathedral city, and glorying in its exemptions granted. and confirmed by Popes, was doubtless an offence in the eyes of the bishop and of his active officials. As Archdeacon of Lincoln he had then a man exactly after his own heart. Thomas, surnamed Wallensis, or the Welchman, had been distinguished as a scholar at Oxford and Paris, and had been brought by the bishop at an early age from the University because, as he writes to him in making the appointment, " he knows no one likely to be equal to him in pastoral discipline." He knows that it will be hard for him to leave his professor's chair, and his Scriptural studies, and to undertake an office in which many will say that he had regard to temporal wealth and dignity; yet, believing that he can do a good work for the Church herein, he solemnly charges him to accept the post[2]. Thus adjured, Thomas did not refuse, but placed his energy, vigour, and learning at the disposal of the great bishop. It was but natural that a man in his position should be ready to try conclusions with a wealthy, and perhaps, somewhat indolent abbot, his neighbour; and natural also, that the vigour of the archdeacon should be supported by the bishop.

<hr>

[2] Ep. Gross. li.

If, indeed, the account in Matthew Paris is to be taken as exact, it would seem that Archdeacon Thomas somewhat courted the fray. A debt was owing from a former Abbot of Bardney to a certain clerk. The succeeding abbot, when pressed for payment, demurred. The archdeacon hearing of the matter, and "desirous to weaken the almost pontifical dignity of the said abbot and his convent, in which they had long rejoiced undisturbed," persuaded the clerk to make a formal complaint to him, telling him that he would recover his money for him by fair means or foul. Accordingly the complaint was made, and the Abbot of Bardney was summoned to appear before the Archdeacon of Lincoln. The abbot pleaded privilege, and would not appear. A second time he did the same; for, says the historian, "he knew a trap was being laid for him, and that the real object was to disturb and weaken his privilege. He had clear enough evidence that if the cause should reach the bishop, which the archdeacon was cunningly seeking, the bishop would be ready to grant him favour only on the ground of the subversion of the liberty of the monks, inasmuch as he had shown himself the general persecutor of all religious bodies, but especially of those who had privileges, whenever he could find an opportunity of attacking them. The bishop, however, summoned the abbot to answer for his manifold excesses. The abbot relying on his first appeal refused to obey the citation, knowing that the bishop was wont to run headlong into passions, and that he was altogether prejudiced in favour of his archdeacon. Upon which the bishop greatly moved and swelling with wrath more than was fitting, at once excommunicated the said abbot as contumacious. The abbot bore this quietly, but humbly preserved the sentence, lest afterwards he might be punished for contempt[3]." The next step, however, was soon taken by the impetuous bishop. He sent a body of visitors to Bardney, and it is said that he chose secular persons, who were rather disposed to insult the monks than to act as real correctors of abuses. The monks, looking upon them more as persecutors than visitors, would not admit them. The visitors were inclined to try to effect an entrance by force; but the porters drove them out of the enclosure, and recommended them, if they desired to return with whole skins, to retreat at once before the people, who were eager to attack them, came against

[3] Matt. Paris, u. s.

them. They went back to their employer, and made the most of the treatment they had received. The bishop in high dudgeon declared that he would bring ruin and confusion on the monastery. Meantime the abbot, casting about for help against so powerful a foe, bethought him, in an unlucky moment, of appealing to the convent of Canterbury, which (the Archiepiscopal See, being at the time vacant) was supposed to have the right of hearing appeals. Grosseteste's reply to this was to summon three Benedictine Abbots to Hertford, and to cause them to depose the Abbot of Bardney, as convicted and contumacious, although, as the Chronicler fairly remarks, he had had no trial and no opportunity of answering for himself. Upon this the Canterbury monks went through the somewhat idle ceremony of solemnly excommunicating the bishop with bell, book, and candle. "Now, when the bishop beheld the letters conveying this sentence, he threw them upon the ground and trode upon them with the utmost contempt, although the lookers on greatly wondered, inasmuch as the figure of St. Thomas was impressed on the waxen seal." And with such a violent passion did he become heated as to say in the hearing of all, "Just so may the monks pray for my soul for ever[4]." The messenger, too, was railed at and ordered to be seized, but when the reverence for his priestly character prevented this, he was driven contumeliously out of the house like a thief. Meantime the king seized upon the temporalities of the vacant abbey, but as his officer appeared to favour the deprived abbot too much, Grosseteste wrote a peremptory letter to the king, bidding him not to interfere with the ecclesiastical power, and warning him of the fate of Uzziah. Thus the Abbot of Bardney was reduced by the vigorous measures of the bishop, nor were those, whose aid he had sought in his difficulties, to fare much better. Grosseteste treated the excommunication pronounced against him by the Canterbury monks with complete contempt; but yet the matter was thought to have sufficient weight in it to draw forth from the Pope a letter, bidding the monks to relax their sentence, and nominating the Archbishop of York and the Bishop of Durham to do so if they refused[5].

The excessive vigour and energy with which Grosseteste proceeded causes a constant wail to rise from the historian, to whom the immunities of monks were dear. "The Bishop of Lincoln, to

<hr>

[4] Matt. Paris, u. s.   [5] Matt. Paris, p. 605.

whom quiet is an unknown thing; whose hand is against every man as every man's hand is against him; another Ishmael, ready to labour with any amount of toil, and to spend money in reckless profusion that he may carry his point[6]." No doubt, indeed, his extraordinary vigour and decision of character led the Bishop of Lincoln to push the assertion of his episcopal rights to the extremest limits. This was remarkably the case on the question of patronage. The bishop boldly denied the absolute right of any layman to present to a benefice. He is only to present if the bishop pleases to accept. To admit any person to an ecclesiastical benefice and cure of souls, or to refuse any person, is the office and work of the bishop alone, *quà* bishop. The king cannot order a bishop to do or not to do an episcopal and spiritual act. Consequently, he cannot order him to institute or not to institute to churches. Let him beware if he usurps such a power, lest he be struck like King Uzziah[7]. That these views about patronage were not mere theory, but were actually carried out by the bishop, we have proof in the following letter: "To the noble,

6 Matt. Paris, p. 688.

7 Gross. Epist. lxxii. See also Burton Annals, Ann. Monast., i. 422.

lord, Philip de Kyme, Robert, Bishop of Lincoln, &c. It seems, doubtless, harsh and severe to you that, under the authority of the council, I have instituted a prior in your house of Kyme; but, in this, I do not intend to derogate in any way from your right, and you ought not to be annoyed at it. For it is no hardship that I have rejected one less suitable, and substituted one more suitable and more useful to you, without prejudicing any right. Are you vexed that in this matter I have not taken counsel with you? But this is neither customary nor necessary. Be assured I have quashed many appointments in monasteries which are in the patronage of our lord the king, and, without at all taking counsel with him, have appointed heads to the same, whom he has accepted and allowed to have possession of the temporal goods. Be ready to follow his example, and receive the prior, whom we have canonically instituted, with all kindness[8]." It was not, however, on all occasions that these questions of patronage were settled between the king and the bishop in altogether an amicable way. In the case of the presentation to the church of Thame a serious dispute arose. The king, by permission of the Pope, presented to it one of his

Gross. Epist. xxx.

chaplains, named John Mansel. The bishop, however, had already given it away. He sent one of his archdeacons to inform the king of this, and declared that if he did not withdraw his nominee he would excommunicate all concerned in the matter. The king, after an outburst of passion, being afraid of the resolute character of the bishop, yielded[9]. The view which the bishop took as to the way in which the king ought to conduct himself towards him as a chief minister of the church, is expressed in the following letter :—" The very meaning of the word *rex* shows that the king has no power to order save what is *right;* but to uphold children that are disobedient to their father against those who are submissive and obedient, what is this but to prefer darkness to light, bitter to sweet, and evil to good ? . . Whoever are excluded from entering the house of the Lord by the ordinary power ecclesiastical, whether this be done justly or unjustly, no power not ecclesiastical can remove the sentence. If on any grounds such a power should attempt it, it would be acting like Uzzah, and stretching forth its hand to the Ark of the Lord. This be far from that power which you wield[1]." It was not in the bishop's open and

[9] Matt. Paris, p. 570.   [1] Gross. Epist. cii.

earnest nature to speak smooth things when he felt strongly; and, in accordance with this, we find that he habitually absented himself from Court, and was not like some of his brother-prelates ever by the the right hand of royalty, looking out for some fortunate windfall of preferment. The king wrote to remonstrate with him on this apparent want of respect, to which Grosseteste replied that, if the weakness of his body and the urgency of the many ecclesiastical affairs which press upon him were considered a good reason, it might be perceived why he could not wait upon his majesty; "and, although it be against modesty to speak of oneself, yet, like St. Paul, I am compelled, 'as a fool,' to speak to your majesty of myself, that I have a true solicitude for your well-being, both temporal and spiritual, desiring not to share your prosperity, but to help towards your salvation by sharing in your troubles whenever they may fall upon you[2]." Grosseteste had, however, one good friend at Court. The queen appears to have been much attached to him. "The earnest devotion of the queen's majesty," writes Adam de Marisco to him, "which, springing from holy friendship with you, the divine mercy hath inclined towards your fatherhood, gives abundant

[2] Gross. Epist. ci.

trust of salutary effects to be wrought by the evangelical ministry of your piety. God be praised for it. We see here a Providential way opened for a great help to the Church in the midst of so many critical dangers[3]." Indeed, King Henry III., whenever he dared, did not scruple to encroach upon the rights and liberties of any of his subjects whether lay or clerical. Always in pressing need of money, he used all expedients to obtain it. He had tried to extract the value of a year's growth of wool from the great Cistercian body, but had been cunningly thwarted by them. The citizens of London, however, and the unfortunate Jews, had been less successful in resisting[4]. At length (1244) a general assembly of the magnates of the kingdom being held at Westminster, the king explained his necessities and urgently pleaded for money. A committee of twelve was appointed,—four bishops, of whom Grosseteste was one, forming part of it. The clerical and lay members were to deliberate separately, but they agreed that they would only act conjointly. The king had procured letters from the Pope to the bishops urgently pressing upon them the duty of helping his needs. Every art was

[3] "Monumenta Franciscan," p. 102.
[4] Matt. Paris, s. a. 1243.

tried by him to make them agree to a subsidy without exacting conditions, and trusting to his promises, which had been so often broken. They would probably have at length yielded had it not been for Grosseteste, who, reminding them of their compact with the lay members of the committee, exhorted them not to divide themselves from them, and brought forward, says Matthew Paris, this theological authority: "It is written, if we be divided, straightway we shall all perish." Upon this the prelates stood firm, and no money was forthcoming unless the king would mend his ways[5].

[5] Matt. Paris, 639, 10.

CHAPTER VII.

GROSSETESTE AS REFORMER.

1238—1244.

Grosseteste's views with respect to Rome—Not cordial with Archbishop Edmund—Appeals to the Legate against him—Differs from him on the law of bastardy—Will not support him in resisting the "Provisions" of Pope Gregory—Welcomes the appointment of Archbishop Boniface—Seeks his help in the matter of the Bishop of Winchester—Previous history of this case—Grosseteste's letter to Archbishop Boniface—Robert de Passelew elected Bishop of Chichester—Examined by Grosseteste and rejected—Grosseteste and the archbishop prepare to go to Lyons to the Pope.

THE bold and energetic character of Grosseteste, which stands out equally distinct, whether he is assailing powerful abuses, or defending the Church against what he considers the unjust aggressions of the lay power, might lead us to expect to find him ranged in vigorous opposition to the great and crying abuse of his day,—the intrusions of the Pope upon the Church of England. But to these, as we have seen, Grosseteste submitted very patiently in the commencement of his episcopate. Fixing his hopes upon Rome to give him the power of which he felt so much need in the work which he had set himself to perform, he was willing to do much to procure the necessary support. His letters to the cardinals are written in the most deferential terms. To Cardinal Giles he writes, that the Church rests upon the Cardinals of the Roman Church, as the world upon its hinges. These are they whom the Psalmist describes as the "foundations of the round world," while the Pope is like the sun in its strength, giving light to the whole world[1]. With these strong views he felt himself unable to act cordially with Archbishop Edmund in his attempts to restrain and resist the overweening claims of Rome. Thus when the primate would not do as he desired in prohibiting an abbot from acting as judge, Grosseteste did not hesitate to take the matter to the Cardinal Legate. "Inasmuch," he writes, "as the Abbot of Croyland, of the Order of St. Benedict, and canonically subject to me, has been constituted by the king Itinerant Justice, and executes his office among the other judges, and your holiness knows

<hr>

[1] Gross. Epist. xxxvi.

most clearly how unfitting this is, and how much opposed to religion and canon law; and, inasmuch as I in my weakness cannot take away this scandal, there is no other remedy to be hoped for but from your holiness. In a similar case I applied to my lord of Canterbury for help, and he declined to do that which I desired. To you then I come as a suppliant, entreating you that you would provide a sufficient remedy to take away so great an abomination from the house of the Lord[2]."

There was another point besides the secular employment of ecclesiastics in which the Bishop of Lincoln differed from the archbishop, and on which he laid as much stress as on the former. In Grosseteste's time a sharp collision had arisen between the canon and statute law on the subject of bastardy. The latter treated all children as illegitimate who were born out of wedlock, and did not permit the subsequent marriage of the parents to legalize pre-nuptial offspring. By the canon law, however, subsequent marriage was held to legitimatize all such children, and to this Grosseteste, with his ardent zeal for the laws and ordinances of the church, strongly adhered. Upon this subject he wrote a long argumentative letter to William de

<hr>

[2] Gross. Epist. lxxxii.

Ralegh, Treasurer of Exeter, in which he denounces in the strongest terms the law which prevents ante-nuptial children from inheriting patrimony. "This," he says, "is a law unfair and unjust, opposed to the law of nature, to the divine law, to the canonical and the civil law[3]."   Consequently, when called upon by the king to act on this law in his diocese, and to make returns of those illegitimate children who were holding the property of their parents, he refused to do so. Of course the object of the civil power was to seize upon the property,—otherwise it would not probably have much concerned itself in the matter,—but the bishop, full of zeal for the Church, would not be made an instrument for helping it. It appears, however, that Archbishop Edmund had conceded the point, and Grosseteste, hearing of this, writes in great perplexity to him for advice. The tone of his letter is kind and respectful. "Although the length of this letter is already wearisome for one so greatly occupied as you are, yet as 'Charity beareth all things,' I wish in addition to inform your fatherhood, that the king and his council wish to compel me, that when in the King's Court there is proposed against one an exception of bastardy, on the ground

3 Gross. Epist. xxiii.

that the person was born before the solemnization of marriage between his parents, I, at the king's command, should inquire in an ecclesiastical court whether this be so, and that I should make a return to the king on the point whether he was born before matrimony or after; and because I refused to make such a return, I have been cited to appear in the king's court to answer this, 'for,' say the king and his council, 'you, with the Bishops, Earls, and Barons of England have agreed to this form.' I earnestly beg therefore that you would be kind enough to inform me by letter whether you have agreed to this inquiry and return, and that you would, if it be so, give me your fatherly counsel as to what is to be done; for if I return in this form to the king, I fear 'to fall into the hands of the living God,' but if I refuse to return, and you have agreed to do so, I don't see how I can escape falling into the hands of man. Unless, therefore, your wisdom can show me an escape from both these mischiefs, I feel convinced that it is better for me to fall into the hands of man from which God can deliver me, than into the hands of God, out of which there is no one that can deliver me[4]." That there should

---

[4] Gross. Epist. xxvi.

be any temporizing or yielding in these matters out of respect for the civil power Grosseteste could not understand. "Are they," he writes on another occasion to the archbishop, " are they sins, or are they not ?   If they be sins, you are called upon to be our brazen wall and a bulwark for our littleness against all persecution. Be, then, a leader in the camp of Israel ; fight the battles of the Lord, as did the brave Judas Maccabæus; put on the whole armour of God, that ye may be able to withstand in the evil day, and having done all to stand[5]." These words might have been, perhaps, more fittingly employed in encouraging the archbishop in another and more important matter than the one to which they were applied.   In the year 1240, Pope Gregory in the midst of his contest with the Emperor, made that assignment of unexampled audacity which gave to the Romans the three hundred benefices which should first fall vacant in the dioceses of Canterbury, Lincoln and Salisbury, and charged the bishops of these Sees not to collate any one until the claims of the Romans were satisfied.   It was then that the archbishop needed the support of an energetic and vigorous nature such as that of Grosseteste ; but Grosseteste made no

<hr>

[5] **Gross. Epist. xxviii.**

sign. Archbishop Edmund, crushed and over-whelmed at the " detestable exaction," as Matthew Paris well calls it, shrank into retirement at Pontigny. Whether the Bishop of Lincoln himself satisfied the Roman greed is doubtful. Perhaps he evaded it to a certain extent by the privilege which he had obtained from the Pope of not providing for any one at his command unless especial mention was made of this privilege; but, at any rate, we have no indignant protest from him on the subject. By and by he will be of quite another mind in this matter. Grosseteste, probably, saw without much regret Archbishop Edmund resign his see, and welcomed with some satisfaction the appoint-ment to the primacy of a man of an entirely different character and temper from the saintly Edmund—the worldly and turbulent Boniface of Savoy. The ground on which Grosseteste would look with satisfaction to the appointment of Boni-face, was his belief that the young and energetic Savoyard would take a bold stand on church grounds against secular and state encroachments. He was in high favour with the Pope. His brother was the commander of the Papal troops, and he himself had great influence in the Papal court. He was, also, uncle to the queen, ever the fast friend of Grosseteste and the High Church party. The first matter in which Grosseteste needed his help was the matter of the bishopric of Winchester. Here the king was grievously invading church privileges and setting at naught church laws. The see had now been vacant for five years since the death of the famous Peter des Roches. Immediately upon its vacancy Grosseteste had written in a most earnest manner to Cardinal Otho, warning him that the king had taken up his abode near Winchester, and was endeavouring by promises and threats to cause the convent to elect his nominee, whom he does not mention by name, but who was in fact no other than William, elect of Valencia, the queen's uncle. He presses upon the cardinal the immense importance of having for this most influential see a learned and vigorous prelate, and follows up his letter by a second, in which he explains that he had not intended so much to condemn any special person as to urge upon the cardinal the general importance of the subject[6]. The king's influence had availed to annul the first election to Winchester, but yet he could not induce the monks to choose William of Provence. They elected William de Ralegh,

[6] Gross. Epist. lx. lxi.

LIFE OF GROSSETESTE.

Page 156.

Bishop of Norwich, who was also accepted by the Pope. Upon this the king, highly indignant, seized on the revenues both of the see of Winchester and the see of Norwich. According to Matthew Paris, he pursued William de Ralegh, who had formerly been his close friend, with inexorable hatred; permitted no one to associate with him; would not allow him to enter his palace at Southwark, and captured the supplies that were being sent to him from Norwich. Whereupon the bishop, "grieving, and harassed by manifold injuries, made his complaint to his fellow-bishops in lamentable guise. Upon which the Bishops of Lincoln, Worcester, and Hereford, moved by piety, and stirred up by zeal for justice, hastened to Reading to chide the king for these things, and to admonish him to correct them[7]." The king, not unnaturally, escaped; but Grosseteste and his fellows were not to be easily put off, and they at length got an interview. Henry was obstinate and angry; and, refusing to yield, sent privately agents to Rome with commission to spend any money to get the election annulled. But the indefatigable bishops followed him from place to place, "hunting out his track like a fugitive," and

7 Matt. Paris, p. 614.

at length finding him at Westminster, they had another stormy scene with him. " They reproached him sharply for the persecution and tyranny which he ceased not, day by day, to exercise against their brother of Winchester. And as they added prayer to prayer, and threats to threats, and were prepared to put his chapel under an interdict, the king sought for a truce and for delay, till his messengers should return from beyond seas, before giving his precise answer; for he hoped, without doubt, that they would effect what he had designed by corrupting the Papal court[6]." William de Ralegh, taking fright at this cessation on the part of his friends, and fearing lest he should be betrayed, went abroad, and by doing so brought, as the historian tells us, the greatest scandal upon the King of England as a persecutor of his best-bishops, and a rewarder of his friends by injuries. It was not, however, at all the case that Grosseteste and his coadjutors had grown cold in the matter. On the contrary, the Bishop of Lincoln, who regarded Ralegh with affection and respect, although he had formerly looked upon him as too secular, and too much inclined to undervalue canon law, now wrote to Boniface, the elect of Canterbury, for help,

<hr>

[6] Matt. Paris, p. 616.

"We thank the Lord Jesus Christ, the chief pastor," he writes, "for that he has provided the church of Canterbury, long destitute of the comfort of pastor, with that blessing. We hope that, after the example of Jesus Christ, the chief pastor, in whom all pastors are one, you will feed the flock committed unto you in wisdom and doctrine, with judgment, also, and justice, as the prophet says, 'strengthening the diseased and healing that which is sick, binding up that which was broken, and bringing again that which was driven away;' and that, 'seeking that which was lost,' you will, when you have found it, bear it back on the shoulders of fortitude. To bring about these and such like things tending to the honour of God, the liberty of the Church, and the salvation of souls, by your care and unwearied labour, under the help of God, I desire, as befits a son of your obedience, according to the power of my littleness, the help of the Holy Spirit assisting, to be an obedient and sedulous co-operator with you as with a most beloved father. And, because working well and laudably finishing it helps very much to be warned beforehand in these things which have to be done, I would not have you ignorant that when the lord Pope admitted and confirmed the demand made for

the lord of Norwich as Bishop of Winchester, and
wrote to the King of England for him, thus confirming that he should restore to him the castles and
manors of the see, the king has hitherto refused to
do it.   Now, if he persists in this purpose, a great
mischief may come to him and the kingdom, since
in this matter he evidently appears to go against
the lord Pope, to whom, besides the fidelity owed
in common by all princes who are the sons of the
Church, he is specially bound to fidelity under a
most severe penalty by the Charter and oaths of
King John, of illustrious memory, his father, as I
believe you know.   As, then, you are specially
bound to provide for the honour and peace and
tranquillity of the king and his kingdom, and above
all things to defend ecclesiastical liberty and the
acts of my lord the Pope, in order that they may
have due effect, I beseech you, with all earnestness,
to provide sufficient remedies by your wisdom
against so many dangers and such imminent discords and troubles; and because, as wisdom testifies, ' happy is the husband of a good wife,' for the
husband is saved by the wife, his heart being
changed by her sweet and healthful persuasion, as
far as my littleness can perceive, it will be well
done if my lady, the Queen of England, your niece,

be diligently advised and persuaded both by letters and messengers from you, to try to change for the better the heart of my lord the king in this matter, according to the prudence given her by God, and to induce him in every way to desist from his purpose, lest your first entrance into England, which may the God of peace make peaceful, be disturbed by discords of this sort, and it should become necessary for you to quarrel with my lord the king immediately on your arrival[9]." This letter sufficiently discloses the ground on which the Bishop of Lincoln welcomed the appointment of Boniface. He hoped to see him act as a vigorous champion in repressing the encroachments of the State, and making the power of the Church unshackled and effective. Nor did he judge wrongly of what the archbishop would be likely to do. Boniface took up the case warmly. He wrote to the king, earnestly praying him to admit the Bishop of Winchester to his favour; and as Henry's schemes had failed with the Pope, and William of Valencia was dead, he succeeded in reconciling the king to William de Ralegh, and inducing him at length to let go his hold of the temporalities of the See. In another matter in which Grosseteste was not less

[9] Gross. Epist. ~~lxxxiii.~~ lxxxvi.

I.

interested, Boniface also took a strong part against
the king, and in support of the rights of the
Church and the wishes of his suffragans [1]. Robert
de Passelew, the forest-judge, on whose account
Grosseteste afterwards came into such strong collision with the archbishop, had been appointed by
the king Bishop of Chichester on the death of
Ralph de Neville. He had been the means of
putting great sums of money into the king's purse,
and Henry was proportionately grateful. The
chapter had yielded to the king's nomination,
but the election would not be valid unless confirmed by the archbishop. Boniface was ready to
refuse, but he required a reason for doing so; and
this Grosseteste, and the bishops who acted with
him, proceeded to furnish him with. The forest-
judge, who had probably spent his time in attending to far other matters, was suddenly summoned
to undergo an examination in theology, and the exa-
miner was to be no other than Grosseteste, the most
abstruse scholar of his day, and who went to his
work of examination by no means inclined to spare
the candidate. We are not much surprised to hear
that the forest-judge being examined " in too difficult points [1]," was declared unfit for consecration,

<hr>

[1] Matt. Paris, p. 652. Annal. Monast., ii. 333.

and thus the archbishop, being furnished with a pretext, refused to confirm the election, and appointed Richard de la Wych, better known in Church history as St. Richard of Chichester.

Grosseteste was thus playing a prominent and influential part in the affairs of the Church at large, while all the time he was carrying on with undiminished vigour the disciplining of his own diocese. The time had now arrived when the long-protracted dispute with his dean and chapter, of which an account has been given in a previous chapter, must be brought to an issue. Pope Innocent had summoned a council to meet at Lyons, principally with the view of carrying on his quarrel with the Emperor Frederick. To that council Boniface, the elect of Canterbury, was about to proceed to seek consecration; and thither, too, did Grosseteste prepare to go, hoping to obtain the final decision of the Pope, with regard to his claim to visit the Dean and Chapter of Lincoln, and the churches belonging to the cathedral.

CHAPTER VIII.

GROSSETESTE AT THE COUNCIL OF LYONS.

1244—1246.

Grosseteste's letter to his archdeacons preparatory to his journey—His reception at Lyons—The Dean of Lincoln made Bishop of Lichfield—Final settlement of the quarrel between the bishop and the chapter—The Pope exacts a payment for his favours —The renewal of the cession of King John—The subsidy for Archbishop Boniface—The tax on England for the Pope—Grosseteste's letter defending it—Protests of the English clergy and nobles against this tax—Grosseteste's letter as to his return.

AMONG the preparations made by the Bishop of Lincoln for his journey to the Papal Court, was a solemn letter or charge addressed to his archdeacons bidding them show an increase of vigilance and earnestness in their work during his absence; the substance of which was as follows: " The man going into a far country gave his goods to his servants, that on his return he might receive them multiplied. This represents prelates obliged to go abroad that they may seek that which was lost, whose goods are the powers and dispensations of the ministry of souls. I then, going abroad for such a reason as I have said, may, in the character of that man, say to you, 'Occupy till I come.' In going to foreign lands, I am in body far separated from the family over which I am placed, but ye are placed over the household to give them their meat in due season. I beseech you by the sprinkling of the blood of Jesus Christ 'Occupy till I come.' Do not lay up the power of the ministry of salvation entrusted to you in the napkin of idleness, but observe the prophet's words, 'Cry aloud, spare not, lift up thy voice like a trumpet[1].' The Son of God, equal to the Father, being in the form of God, in order to save souls, made Himself of no reputation and took on Him the form of a servant, and endured all things, even to the death upon the Cross. Do you who stand in His place for this work follow in His footsteps, undeterred by earthly terror, and uninfluenced by earthly love. The hired servant receives wages for his work; but if he is negligent and careless he receives no pay.

[1] Isaiah lviii. 1.

and is liable to account for any damage that may have happened through his fault. To you is given the work of converting souls; but your wages will not be paid to you except you do your work, and you will be liable to account for any loss that may happen. If any souls committed to your charge, shall by your negligence be deprived of the effect of the Lord's passion, that is, eternal salvation, do ye not make the death of Christ of none effect, as far as they are concerned? Do ye not also keep back the completion of the number of those who are to be saved, and thus cause the delay of the general resurrection of the dead, and the renewal of the world, the last judgment, and the kingdom prepared for the saints from the beginning of the world, and thus injure that whole creation which groaneth and travaileth in pain until now, waiting for the manifestation of the sons of God. What can be the expectation of such, except that the creation serving its Maker should 'increase its strength against the unrighteous for their punishment[2]?' and how will any one be able to endure to be tortured by universal creation, to whom the burning of even one spark is intolerable?"

With such solemn and awful words did the bishop

[2] Wisdom xvi. 24.

leave his last charge to his archdeacons when he went on his way to that which he held to be a solemn and pressing duty.

The bishop started from England for Lyons on November 18, in company with his friend Adam de Marisco, and some other friars, and reached Lyons on January 7, 1245. He himself records the fact that he was received by the Pope and cardinals "in a sufficiently becoming and honourable way[3]." Adam de Marisco, in a letter to the Superior of the Franciscans in England, speaks somewhat more strongly:—"The Lord of Lincoln, with his party, reached Lyons on the morrow of the Epiphany, in better health than usual, and was received by the Pope and cardinals with the favour of special honour. The lord Pope promised him, a few days after, that he would shortly expedite him in his cause against his chapter, which we hope, with the divine blessing, will be concluded favourably, unless our sins hinder it. Yet the event of war is doubtful to mortals: for there is no cessation of impious plots, shuffling, cunning, and delay, to hinder the advance of that which is salutary. The bishop proposes to attend the council which the lord Pope agrees to celebrate at the Feast of

[3] Gross. Epist. cxiii.

St. John the Baptist, and to wait till that time in some place, not in the Court, being altogether ignorant when he shall be able to leave the Court[4]." But before the council began Grosseteste's great matter was (to him) satisfactorily settled. William de Monte Pezzulano, who had been elected Bishop of Lichfield and Coventry, was distasteful to King Henry, who had refused his confirmation of the choice of the chapter, and had also pressed to have the election annulled by the Pope. The bishop-elect not seeing any probability of overcoming the difficulties thus put in his way, had signified to the Pope that he resigned his claim. The resignation was gladly welcomed, as it gave an opportunity to the Pope of making a bishop, who, deriving immediately from him, would be his willing helper in England; and to the Bishop of Lincoln it came opportunely, as opening a way by which the Dean of Lincoln, his nominal opponent, could be comfortably provided for, on his giving up that which had cost so many years of strife, and such vast expense, and which had now caused his own journey to Lyons, viz. the claims of his chapter. It is true the clergy of the diocese of Lichfield, as represented by the chapter, had no opportunity of

4 "Monumenta Franciscana," p. 376.

expressing their opinion, although the right to elect was solemnly guaranteed to them by Magna Charta. It is true the king was not applied to, to order the confirmation, although this too was his undoubted privilege, and he at any rate deserved to be considered by the Pope, to whom he had done such great favours. These considerations were not allowed to stand in the way of so very advantageous an arrangement, and so, under the auspices of a Pope who was not much troubled by scruples when his own interests were concerned, the long quarrel between the bishop and the Chapter of Lincoln was at length arranged. Roger de Wescham, Dean of Lincoln, was consecrated Bishop of Lichfield, and immediately afterwards the suit between Grosseteste and the dean and canons was determined almost entirely in favour of the bishop. It has been justly remarked on this transaction :—
" However much one might wish to think differently, it is difficult not to suspect unfair dealings between the bishop and the dean. In the first place the dean, Roger de Wescham, is Grosseteste's intimate friend; he is sent by the chapter to represent them and plead their cause. He has not been at Lyons more than a few weeks, when, by Grosseteste's influence, he is elected Bishop of Lich-

field, and immediately afterwards Grosseteste gains from the Pope a Bull giving him all he asks for against the chapter. It is difficult not to suspect that a bargain was struck between these two. If Wescham really felt that the claims of the chapter were altogether wrong, why did he go out as their representative[5]?"

A Bull of Pope Innocent IV., dated August 25, 1245, provided as follows :—

1. The bishop is invested with the power of visiting the dean and chapter, the prebendal churches, the churches of the dignitaries, and those belonging to the corporate body, as ordinary; and the dean's ordinary power is taken away.

2. The power to correct irregularities in the persons attached to the cathedral is allowed to the chapter, but if they do not correct them the bishop may interfere and cause it to be done.

3. The canons are to pay canonical obedience and reverence to the bishop; but they are not to be required to take an oath to this effect, that being contrary to precedent.

Other points which had been urged by the bishop,—such as the payment of procurations when he visited, his solemn reception with ringing of

[5] Luard's Preface to Grosseteste's Letters, p. 62.

bells, the power to sequestrate on a vacancy, the necessity of his granting his licence before an election,—were dismissed by the Pope, whose wish evidently was to keep up to a certain extent the special and peculiar position of the chapter, and who was not prepared to go to the full length of Grosseteste's claim, which aimed at putting the cathedral exactly on the same footing as any of the parish churches of his diocese[6]. The bishop was now also permitted by the Pope to detach the prebend of Aylesbury from the deanery of Lincoln, on the ground, as Matthew Paris says, that its immense value caused the dean to hold his horns too high and to kick against the bishop[7]. Such were the bishop's gains from Pope Innocent at Lyons; but now for the price which he paid for them. A Pope, such as Innocent IV., does not scatter favours for nothing; he takes care to secure at least an equivalent; and in this case Grosseteste, indeed, paid far more than an equivalent. In his great and absorbing desire for power—power which was designed, indeed, for the most excellent uses— he sacrificed patriotism, the care for the liberties of the English Church, the due regard for the interests of his brother clergy, and the respect which he

6 Matt. Paris, p. 689.   7 Matt. Paris, p. 661.

owed to the king and the State. Blinded by his prosperous advance, he seems to have forgotten all but complete devotion to the Pope, and to have been only desirous to testify his entire and unhesitating gratitude. The English bishops who had asembled at Lyons to attend the council were all more or less personally bound to the Pope, and he determined to use them by making them join in an act which cannot but be considered disgraceful to those who consented to it.

The instrument by which King John had pretended to make over his kingdom to the Roman bishop had lately been accidentally destroyed by fire. Upon this the Pope had caused a new deed to be prepared, and, in order to support it, he required all the English bishops who were present at Lyons to put their signatures to it. We must give the very words of Matthew Paris, which do him much honour :—" The Pope sent a message to each of the English bishops, charging them most urgently that each of them should set his seal to that detestable document, which John of wretched memory, King of the English, in spite of the protests of Stephen, Archbishop of Canterbury, unfortunately drew up on the subject of paying tribute to Rome, in order that being the more

strengthened it might be perpetuated. And this
the bishops, being most inexcusably demoralized
by fear, did, to the enormous injury, alas! both of
the king and the kingdom[8]!" It seems almost
incredible that the bishop who afterwards displayed
such a noble independence and strength of character, should have put his hand to this charter of
degradation; but at this moment he was probably
doing much out of deference for others, which in
his heart he could not approve. He was compromised by his connexion with Boniface, a man
utterly without scruples, but who, as yet, attracted
Grosseteste because he seemed earnestly bent upon
exalting the power of the Church. He was compromised also by the other bishops with whom he had
been acting. These were Walter de Cantilupe,
Bishop of Worcester, the defender of pluralities at
the Council of London, an outspoken champion of
abuses, and Peter d'Aquablancâ, Bishop of Hereford, a man of no character, ready to sell any thing
or any body. These two, says Matthew Paris,
were among all the bishops of England the most
devoted to the Pope and the most hated by the
people[9]. Yet with these men Grosseteste had been
acting in the matter of the Bishop of Winchester,

<hr>

[8] Matt. Paris, p. 681.　　　　　[9] Matt. Paris, p. 653.

and with them he now joined in the consecration of Boniface at Rome[1]. He joined them too, it is to be feared, in encouraging the Pope to resist and despise the representations and remonstrances poured into the Lyons Council by the nobles of England and the king, as to the "execrable extortions" of the Pope. "The conduct of the bishops," says Dr. Hook, "was extremely disgraceful. Those who obeyed the summons to the council were over-awed and intimidated. Even such men as Grosseteste succumbed. They were carried away by that professional feeling which had little influence upon them in England[2]."

The Bishop of Lincoln was soon made to feel that the friendship of Boniface could not be had without its price. Although the new archbishop had gone from England to Lyons enriched with the spoils of his see, yet the first thing that he sought from the Pope on his arrival was a power to extort large contributions from the whole of his province. So eager was he to raise these that, immediately upon his consecration, he sent to Grosseteste two of his clerks, to ask him to affix his seal to letters to

[1] See the Note in Dr. Hook's "Lives of the Archbishops," vol. iii. p. 247.

[2] "Lives of the Archbishops," iii. 246.

be sent at once to England enforcing the Pope's grant of a subsidy to the see of Canterbury. The Bishop of Lincoln had not at that time resided long enough in the midst of the intrigues and machinations of the Papal Court to be able to grant so astounding a request. He still had some feeling for the oppressed and pillaged Church at home, and he responded to Boniface's request with a letter which is conceived in a fitting spirit. He declares that if he yielded to the archbishop's request he should "render himself odious to the whole clergy of the province, who might publicly proclaim that as far as he was concerned, by this premature concession, he had loaded them with an intolerable burden[3]."

It is sad, however, to have to chronicle the fact that the good reasons which he gave for not joining with the archbishop in his exactions ceased to weigh with Grosseteste, when, after a little time, his own affair with the chapter had been satisfactorily settled. He then saw things in a different light, and was ready to lend the weight and authority of his name to this heavy and causeless tax in favour of the archbishop. On the 27th of August (1245), two days after the decree in Grosseteste's favour as against his chapter was given, came

[3] Gross. Epist. lxxxix.

forth a formal letter in which Robert, Bishop of Lincoln, certifies that he has seen and inspected certain letters of the Pope granting to the Archbishop of Canterbury, on account of the debts of his see, the sum of ten thousand marks to be raised from the first-fruits of all the benefices in the Province which should fall vacant during the next seven years, the tax to be collected by the Bishop of Hereford, and to be applied to the discharge of these debts[4]. This tax for Archbishop Boniface seems to have been excessive and unjustifiable, yet, at any rate, it was English—for an English see, for English purposes. It was not so, however, with the other money transactions in which Grosseteste was now engaged. He, who had withstood so boldly the king's exactions, is now converted into the Pope's tax-gatherer; and the gatherer of a tax for the Pope having perhaps the least colour of right of any that he demanded, the pretence namely, of carrying on his war against the emperor. Upon the king remonstrating with him upon his return to England for doing this, he replied in a letter which clearly sets forth the principles which at this time guided his conduct. These principles are, indeed, utterly distasteful to our modern ideas,

---

[4] Matt. Paris, p. 692.

but they were honestly held by Grosseteste, and, when he himself was brought to see the mischief of them, as honestly repudiated.

"Your majesty has written to me that you are astonished not a little and much moved that I propose personally to assess and collect the tax for our lord the Pope from religious men and clerks. May it please you, therefore, to know that I do not act in this matter by myself, nor alone; my brother bishops are doing or have done the same, compelled as I am by the authority and command of the sovereign Pontiff, whom not to obey is the sin of witchcraft and idolatry. It is not then a matter for astonishment that we deal in this matter; much rather would it be a matter for astonishment and indignation if, even without being asked or commanded, we should not be ready to do a thing of this sort or even a greater thing. We see our spiritual father and mother suffering affliction, and were we not to help them in such a state, we should be transgressing the commandments of the Lord, we should be throwing away the fear of the Lord and forfeiting His blessing[5]." Happily there were in England at that day some clergy possessed of a more independent spirit than Grosseteste had as

____
[5] Gross. Epist. cvi.

yet arrived at, and more akin to that which in a few years he would reach. The demand of the Pope was so enormous that it amounted to no less than a half of all ecclesiastical revenues for three years, wherever the holder of the benefice had not resided six months in the year. In some other cases it reached a third part, and in some others a twentieth. Upon this demand being made, an assembly of the nobles and clergy was held at Westminster, and the clergy drew up a paper of objections and answers to the demand[6]. They urge that to take away half of all the revenues of non-residents would bear very hard upon canons of cathedrals, who hold a number of churches, but out of their rents support the under-officers of the church. Also, that the monasteries which hold the tithes of many churches would be reduced to beggary by this demand. Also they say, "inasmuch as in this kingdom of England it has hitherto been the custom that the rectors of parish churches have been very hospitable, and have been wont to support their poorer parishioners, and by so doing have acted in a way pleasing to God as well as to men; if they lose the half of their benefices they

[6] Printed in Burton Annals, Ann. Monast., i. 220, and Matt. Paris, p. 716.

will be obliged to withdraw their hospitality, and will thus incur the anger and ill-will of their people. They will be compelled to give up their religious duties and the services of the church, while those who have been wont to be supported by them will either starve or take to robbery. The many clerks, also, who are much in debt, if their debts be not taken into consideration in calculating the half, and also the expense of collecting their revenues, will be utterly ruined. The sum demanded would amount to not less than 80,000 marks, a sum which the whole kingdom would be unable to furnish. On these grounds the Church of England solemnly refuses it, and appeals to a General Council.[7] " The letter of the nobles on the same subject is a wholesome comment upon Grosseteste's words about being obliged to reverence our Mother the Church and our Father the Pope. " The mother ought to remember the children of her womb, and if she does not so, but withdraws their food and milk from them, she seems to be a step-mother. The father who is not kind towards his children is not a father." They then state their grievances :—

1. The Pope is not satisfied with St. Peter's

[7] Ann. Monast., i. 280.

penny, but extorts a heavy contribution from the clergy of England, without the consent of the king, and against the ancient customs.

2. Churches are not left to their lawful patrons to present, but Romans are intruded into them, who carry away all their revenues into other lands.

3. The Pope has broken his promise in the matter of limiting the number of provisions.

4. In the same benefice one Italian succeeds another, so that absolutely nothing is done for the parish.

5. General taxes are assessed and collected without the assent and permission of the king, and in spite of the appeal of his proctors and the opposition of the whole kingdom.

6. "Since the arrival of that infamous nuncio[8]" the clause *non obstante* has been introduced into documents, which is simply an overthrowing of all solemn oaths, arrangements, and provisions.

7. The Italians do nothing for the churches and parishes, but let all go to absolute decay[9].

This is the true description of that system, which the Bishop of Lincoln, so zealous for the souls of his flock, deliberately defended and upheld, be-

[8] Martin.   [9] Ann. Monast., i. 284.

lieving, as he did, in the paramount rights of the Pope over all ecclesiastical revenues. In spite of the opposition of the king, the nobles, and the clergy, the Papal exactions appear to have been successful, and the "gapings of Roman avarice," as Matthew Paris calls them, were satisfied[1].

A letter, written by the bishop on his return journey, is interesting, as illustrating the tender and affectionate side of his character, which was especially brought out toward his beloved Franciscan friars, who had, doubtless, been his advisers and supporters through all these measures. It is addressed to William of Nottingham, the chief of the English Franciscans:—"True friends are not troubled but rather consoled by all that is done by Him Whom we embrace in true friendship, and, as you are a true lover and friend of God, nothing which He ordains can vex you. It has then come to pass in His providence that brother John, the companion of brother Adam, is attacked by a quartan fever, with which he was first taken at Beaune, on our way back. We brought him, with frequent rests, to Nogent, and thence sent him down by the Seine to Paris; and inasmuch as he was neither able to follow us thence to the sea, nor to stay in

1 Matt. Paris, p. 709.

Paris on acount of the bad air, we determined that he should go on by water to Rouen, brother Adam bearing him company, who was not willing to leave him till he had put him in the hands of some brothers whom he knew, in a healthy spot, and whose plan was, after doing this, to meet me at the sea. At Mantes, however, the said brother John getting much weaker, brother Adam could not take him any further nor leave him. Both of them, therefore, have remained at Mantes, and I earnestly entreat you to send Peter of Tewkesbury[2], with some brethren, who can stay with brother John till he is better, and Peter and Adam can return together. This both the brethren wish for. Indeed it is not safe that brother Adam should stay long in these parts, for there are many who wish to keep him at Paris,—Alexander de Hales and John de Rupellis being dead; but if this were to happen both you and I should be robbed of our greatest comfort. Let the said Peter be sure to see me before he sails. I hope, God willing, to be at the Isle of Wight the Saturday after the feast of St. Dionysius. As regards the cause of the visitation, blessed be God, there has been a clear decision

---

[2] Probably mentioned as having special skill in medicine.

given in my favour, and consequently in that of all the bishops[3]."

With these feelings of triumph and satisfaction Grosseteste returned to prosecute the arduous work of correction and reformation in his vast diocese. He came back thoroughly committed to the extremest Papal obedience, to collect the Pope's taxes, to carry out his policy, to be the dutiful officer of his court. We have now to chronicle his gradual recoil from this state of slavish obedience. The recoil was forced upon a soul—which loved righteousness in spite of fallacies which had been long accepted as principles—by the inherent viciousness of the system he was pledged to help forward. Soon the prelate, now all deference and submission, stands again in the same place where his unhappy compliances had been made, and, with withering scorn and words of fire, denounces that court which now he venerated, and breaks in pieces the idol which he had worshipped.

3 Gross. Epist. cxiv.

CHAPTER IX.

GROSSETESTE CHANGING TOWARDS THE PAPAL SYSTEM.

1246—1250.

Change beginning in Grosseteste's views towards Rome—His severe visitation of the laity stopped by the king—He visits the prebendal churches—Begins to find out the real character of Archbishop Boniface—Refuses to institute R. de Passelew to a living—Refuses his support to two friars who were collecting money for the Pope—The Sacred Blood—Grosseteste's explanation—Protest against the king's unjust dealings—Case of the clerk Ralph and the Sheriff of Rutland—The Pope interferes—Visitation at Dunstable and Caudwell—The Exempt Orders—Grosseteste determines to take measures againstthem—Determines to resist the archbishop's exactions—Goes a second time to Lyons—Description from Matthew Paris of his proceedings there.

CONVINCED as Grosseteste was that the Church, above all things, needed a powerful disciplinary law, and convinced as he also was that this law must proceed from the Church itself, not from the State, which could not, in his view, without sacrilege, touch things sacred, it is not to be wondered at that in his zeal for the house of God, he looked up with profound deference to the then universally recognized head of the Church and fountain of its law—the Pope. But he could not have remained for the time which he did in the Papal court,—he could not have witnessed the plots and machinations, the low cunning and pretences, there prevalent, without being morally revolted. Even the questionable transactions with which he himself had been mixed up must have troubled his conscience, and when he returned home the change soon became apparent. True, he collected the tax for the Pope, and defended it stoutly against the king's remonstrance; but, when he saw every where the marks of the mischief the Papal system was working,—above all, when he saw, according to the Pope's Provisions, aliens not caring for the flock enjoying the benefices designed to promote the salvation of souls, then his anger and vexation began to appear. Matthew Paris, speaking of a somewhat later period, says, " he had learned to hate those rascally Romans who had the Papal rescript for Provision, as the poison of a serpent.

He was in the habit of saying that if he should commit the care of souls to them, he should be acting the part of Satan[1]." Doubtless this salutary knowledge was beginning to be acquired soon after his return from the Council of Lyons, for now the indefatigable bishop was more active than ever in his work of visitation. The king, not over well pleased with him for standing between him and the pockets of his subjects, while he freely collected the tax of the Pope, showed his vexation by endeavouring to hinder Grosseteste's searching inquisition. It was Grosseteste's opinion that the cause of ecclesiastical discipline might be legitimately advanced by laymen being called before the bishop and obliged to purge themselves upon oath from an imputed crime. In his view, " bishops and archdeacons have the pastoral care, not only of the clergy, but also of the people, and for this reason are bound by their pastoral office to visit not only the clergy, but the people also ; and, inasmuch as the office of visitation cannot fittingly be fulfilled without the most exact inquisitions, in which it is often necessary to put the oath to those who are concerned in the inquisition[2]." In

[1] Matt. Paris, p. 826.
[2] Annal. de Burton, Ann. Monast., i. 423.

accordance with this view we have it recorded by Matthew Paris that he acted so rigorously in calling the laity before him and putting them to their purgation, that he brought out the interference of the king, which for once appears to have been successful. " At this time," says Matthew Paris, " the Bishop of Lincoln was raging against his subjects more than was fitting or expedient, at the suggestion, as it is said, of the Friars-Preachers and Minors. To such an extent, indeed, did he proceed, that he made strict inquisitions through the archdeacons and deans of his see, concerning the continence and morals, both of noble and ignoble, to the immense injury of the character of many, and great scandal. Then the lord king hearing the heavy complaints of the people, by the advice of his court, wrote to the Sheriff of Hertfordshire thus: 'We command you, as you love yourself and yours, that you should not permit any laymen in your county to be assembled at the pleasure of the Bishop of Lincoln, his archdeacons, officials, and rural deans, to make inquiries of them by their oath and attestations, except it be in causes of matrimony and testamentary causes;' which when the bishop heard, he asserted that the lord king was about to follow the steps of those in France who had already broken faith with similar audacity[3]."

The bishop having now obtained the power of visiting the churches attached to the cathedral, as well as others in his diocese, was not likely to let his new authority lie dormant. Accordingly, we find him without delay employed in visiting the prebends. He had originally intended to visit the cathedral in the first place, and then pass on to the prebends; but at the request of the dean, Henry de Lexington, who had succeded Weseham, he changed his plan, and began with the prebends in the archdeaconry of Stow. For this he was severely attacked, and accused of "mendacity, inconstancy, and imprudence." The dean appears to have joined in the remonstrance, though, as Grosseteste reminds him, the change had been made at his request[4]. No doubt, by critics so unfriendly as the defeated chapter, every movement of the bishop would be captiously scanned. When Grosseteste arrived at Lincoln, he saw by the looks of the canons that their passions had been much stirred up against him, but he appeals

[3] Matt. Paris, p. 716. The reference is to a conspiracy of some French nobles against the Pope, on account of his exactions.

[4] Gross. Epist. cxxi.

to their reason and justice not to allow frivolous motives to influence them[5]. This letter may have produced some good effect, but whether the canons were mollified into respectful deference, or still held aloof from him and threw impediments in his way, Grosseteste was not the man to attach much importance to their attitude in a matter where he believed he saw his duty clearly. The discipline and efficiency of the Church was with him a paramount consideration. His determination to carry this out at all hazards, soon brought him into collision with the prelate whom he had so substantially aided, and by whose side he had so long stood—Archbishop Boniface. It is singular that the beginning of his variance with the archbishop arose in the matter of the same person against whom they had formerly acted cordially together. Robert de Passelew was too useful a feeder of the exchequer as forest-judge, to be neglected by the king. He had failed to procure for him the bishopric of Chichester through the opposition of the archbishop and Grosseteste; he now conferred on him the vicarage of St. Peter's, Northampton. Robert had previously held two livings in the diocese of Lincoln, much, no doubt, to the bishop's

[5] Gross. Epist. cxxii.

annoyance, who considered that the duties of a forest-judge[6] were not compatible with those of the cure of souls. Accordingly he determined vigorously to resist this new appointment.

He wrote to the king:—" Concerning your highness's demand as to a clerk presented by you to a certain church, we would specially inform you that we have given answer to the Lord Robert de Passelew, presented to the church of St. Peter, Northampton, out of our paternal care for his salvation, and that of the souls of the said parish, acting tranquilly and in a spirit of mildness, that so long as he holds the office of forest-judge, we would not commit to him the care of souls, inasmuch as we could not do this except in opposition to the divine law, and the canonical scriptures, and our own profession at our consecration[7]" This decided refusal was not, as may be supposed, very palatable to the king. Upon this the bishop wrote a letter of the tenor usual in such cases.

[6] "The duty of his office is to inquire judicially concerning theft of venery and vert in the king's forest, and to cause those who are convicted of those offences to be taken and incarcerated, whether they be laymen or clerks" (Gross. Epist. p. 353). *Vert, viridis,* is defined by Ducange to be "any green thing which might hide or cover a deer."

[7] Gross. Epist. cxxiv.

He is very sorry if he has offended, his devotion to the king is great, but he has no intention of yielding in the matter in dispute[8]. It would seem that on this the king applied to Archbishop Boniface to institute over the head of his suffragan, and the archbishop, who was not much fettered by considerations of justice and right, authorized his official to act in the matter. This drew forth a letter of remonstrance from Grosseteste to the archbishop. The bishop was prepared to fight the battles of the Church, when he saw a great principle to be at stake. The reasons which had originally attached him to Boniface, namely the presumed help which he could obtain from his influence in his arduous labours, would no longer hold good if the archbishop was merely to be the king's instrument for unjust exactions, and we shall soon see Grosseteste ranged in more direct opposition to the arbitrary and grasping proceedings of the Primate.

In every way we can now trace the progress of the reaction in Grosseteste's views against the false position into which he had been led on his first visit to Lyons. Then he had consented to gather the Pope's tax, and had done so in spite of remonstrance from king and nobles. Now, a

---

[8] Gross. Epist. cxxv.

year later, he can see what gross exactions these Papal levies are, and when two of the Pope's emissaries visit him to engage his help in collecting six hundred marks from his diocese for the Pope, they find no favourable reception. Minorites though they were, and "armed with many Papal Bulls," the bishop did not hesitate to tell them that "this exaction of theirs was a thing not to be heard of, and altogether disgraceful, and impossible to be satisfied." And he added that he spoke not for himself alone but for "the whole clergy and people and all estates of the realm[9]."

In the same year (1247) Grosseteste's diocesan labours were interrupted by a curious incident, the narration of which in Matthew Paris illustrates remarkably the religious England of that day. A summons had been despatched by King Henry to all the great men of the land, to meet him in London on the day of the translation of St. Edmund, when, as they were told, they should hear some tidings of most joyous import. Many responded to so pleasing an invitation, and when they inquired the nature of the good news, they were told that the king had just received the precious gift of a vessel containing the true blood

9 Matt. Paris, p. 722.

of the Saviour, and that he desired in a solemn way to do it honour, and at the same time to honour the royal saint whose glorious church rose at Westminster. The genuineness of the holy blood brought by a distinguished Templar from the sacred land, was certified by the seals of the Masters of the Templars and the Hospitallers, the Patriarch of Jerusalem, and many bishops and abbots. It was contained in a crystal vase of great beauty, and given to Henry as the most religious king of Europe. Such a present could not but kindle the royal enthusiasm to the utmost. Accordingly, at St. Paul's church, where a large body of bishops and priests, clad in their most splendid copes, were assembled, the king, receiving the vase with profound veneration, proceeded to carry it, held aloft in honour, in solemn procession from St. Paul's to Westminster, and after perambulating the abbey, to bestow it on the church of St. Peter at Westminster, on St. Edward and the holy Chapter. The Bishop of Norwich said Mass, and in an address exalted the treasure of the Holy Blood above that of the Cross, which was possessed by the king of France. Some, however, were heard to mutter an objection, and to suggest that as Christ rose truly from the grave with His body perfect, how could His blood be there in a separate state[1]? This brought out the great theologian of the day, the Bishop of Lincoln, who then and there determined the question. In a discourse which has been preserved by Matthew Paris, who was present, Grosseteste demonstrated that there were two kinds of blood,—one, which is produced from the nutriment taken by the body, which may be poured out in greater or lesser quantities without the life being affected. Of this natural blood of Christ was that which was contained in the vase. The other sort which is the very substance of the living body, called by Moses the life of the body, is wholly with the Saviour in heaven, so far as we know. The bishop further showed that there was a difference between the resurrection of the bodies of the faithful and the body of our Saviour. The faithful will rise glorified and relieved from all wound, imperfection of form, &c., but Christ rose with His wounds for highly important purposes, to confirm the faith of the disciples, and to demonstrate His own omnipotence[2].

The king, who took so devout a part in this religious ceremonial, was indeed an admirable disciple of the Pharisees. He showed the utmost external religion,

[1] Matt. Paris, 735-6.   [2] Matt. Paris, Addit. 161-3.

but he neglected justice and judgment, and the weightier matters of the law. He could carry the holy vase in procession with the most edifying demeanour, but he scrupled not to harass his subjects with a perpetual series of gross and fraudulent oppressions. At this time occurred one of those solemn protests and remonstrances against his grievous malversations, which were continually going on during his reign, and which at length issued in the Barons' War. Although there is no direct evidence to show that Grosseteste took a prominent part in resenting and striving to redress the oppressions practised on the people, yet from the fact of his having been present at the Parliament held this year at Westminster[3] (1248) we are perhaps justified in connecting his name with the remonstrance then made. The king was sharply reminded when he asked for a subsidy, that when the last subsidy was granted he had given his solemn undertaking that he would cease from his malpractices. Nevertheless he had been since that time more than ever busy in bringing in aliens and marrying them to English heiresses; he had grievously oppressed the tradesmen by taking from them their wares without payment; even the poor fishermen had

[3] Matt. Paris, p. 743.

N 2

been robbed of their fish for the royal table. Another complaint was added in which the Bishop of Lincoln would certainly join. The king was charged with keeping bishoprics and abbacies vacant, and perverting their revenues to his own uses[4]. Of course the king made promises of amendment, but no one trusted him, and but small respect could have been felt, by any of those who tried to do their duty, towards one who so grossly outraged all the laws of justice and truth. In the vigorous administration of discipline which he held to be of the most vital importance to the Church, Grosseteste would not be willing to stay his hand on account of one who so ill performed his own obligations. The king had showed that it was but of little use to expect the pure administration of the law from him, and in the matter of Robert de Passelew, John Mansell the Bishop of Winchester, and others, had proved that he had but scant respect for the privileges of the Church when it suited him to trample upon them. Probably this was the reason which led Grosseteste to take the law into his own hands as he did in the matter of the Sheriff of Rutland—a proceeding not justifiable perhaps on ordinary grounds, but, it may be, ex-

<hr>

[4] Matt. Paris, p. 744.

cusable under the circumstances. A clerk named Ralph, accused of incontinence, had been excommunicated by the bishop. As he did not submit within forty days, the bishop charged the Sheriff of Rutland to imprison him. The sheriff refused, and he too at once incurred the sentence of excommunication. At this, the king highly incensed at a royal officer being thus treated, appealed to Rome, and Grosseteste was now to learn that all the compliances which he had made to the Pope, and all the zeal with which he had promoted his interests in collecting money for him even against the edicts of the king, would not suffice to prevent his being immediately thrown over when the Pope's interests seemed to point that way. The king obtained a rescript from Pope Innocent, forbidding bishops to carry on processes by means of the king's officers, and to use excommunication against them if they failed to act[5]. This direction may have been a very salutary one, but it was hardly what the Bishop of Lincoln would expect at the hands of the Pope, and it was without doubt one of the matters which influenced him to prepare a second time to visit Lyons—a visit from which such important consequences flowed. Other trains of

[5] Matt. Paris, p. 777.

circumstances connected with his episcopal work were leading him to the same point. In the year 1249 he visited the priory of Dunstable, and the priory of Caudwell, and in both of these houses found matter needing correction. In the first-named the cellarer, Henry de Bilendâ, in the second the prior, fearing the discipline of the bishop, withdrew from their respective houses and took refuge in the Cistercian Monastery of Merivale in Warwickshire[6]. Once with Cistercians the bishop had no power to touch them. The White Monks, strong in their oft-confirmed exemptions from diocesan control, could laugh at his threats. But though the bishop could not enter a Cistercian house as visitor, yet there was a point on which he could make even the Cistercians feel his power, and this was a point held by him to be of vital importance, and one which he was determined at all hazards to press to the uttermost. By the rule of the Cistercians, religious houses of their Order were not permitted to hold tithes of churches. But this rule had been altogether disregarded. The White Monks had become impropriators, holders of advowsons, farmers of tithes, just as extensively as their black brethren, and Grosseteste, ever intent

<hr>

[6] Ann. Dunstab., Ann. Monast., iii. 178.

on establishing and permanently endowing vicarages, determined to bring the Papal authority to
bear upon them in this matter. He had obtained
a general authority from the Pope to forbid the
religious houses appropriating tithes without the
consent of him and his chapter; and he now proceeded to act upon this, and his own authority as
diocesan, to inquire into the state of affairs[7]. Accordingly he issued a general summons to all the
monasteries in his diocese to exhibit their charters
before him. "In the same year, 1249," says the
Dunstable annalist, "the Bishop of Lincoln caused
all the religious who held benefices in the diocese of
Lincoln to be summoned, first at Stamford,
secondly at Leicester, thirdly at Oxford, to appear
before him to exhibit the charters of their founders,
the confirmations of bishops, and the Papal privileges. And these being exhibited he retained a
copy of them all for himself, saying that he would
consult the lord Pope upon them[8]." Yet another
cause conduced to make it necessary for the bishop
to go to Lyons to the Pope.

In the matter of Robert de Passelew, Archbishop
Boniface had already shown that he had but slight

<hr>

[7] Matt. Paris, Additamentu, p. 179.
[8] Ann. Monast., iii. 180.

regard for his former friends in his dealings with the Church. But this grievance was not the only one which Grosseteste had against him. This prelate of unblushing effrontery, without taking the trouble himself to visit England, immediately after his consecration commenced a series of extortions by means of his officers, who, under a pretence of visitation in the divers dioceses of the province, exacted large payments. Grosseteste's eyes now seem to have been opened. Although he was prepared to go almost any length to procure more efficient church discipline and the redress of abuses, yet when those who should have redressed abuses appeared as upholding them, he did not hesitate for a moment to take his stand against them. He was determined vigorously to oppose the exactions and oppressions of Archbishop Boniface, and he felt the more bound to do this as his own example had been alleged as a precedent by the archbishop for visiting the Canons of St. Paul's, and other violent measures which he had taken. On all these grounds, then, the Bishop of Lincoln prepared again to visit the Papal Court, and in Lent of 1250[9], in company with many barons of England,

[9] The Dunstable Annals might be interpreted so as to put this journey of Grosseteste to the Lent of 1249; but they will bear the interpretation which gives it to 1250, and this is shown to be the right date from other sources.

LIFE OF GROSSETESTE.   *Page 201.*

full of the unjust oppressions of the king—the
Bishops of London and Worcester, who had their
grievances against Archbishop Boniface to urge—
and attended by his Archdeacons of Oxford and
Bedford and many other clerks, he arrived at
Lyons. The bishop's eyes had already been in
some measure opened to the real character of the
Papal Court, but this visit was happily destined to
dispel all obscurity and to reveal at once and for
ever to him the hopeless corruption and rotten-
ness of the source from which he had long hoped
to draw vigorous and healthy ecclesiastical life.
He himself is freely accused by Matthew Paris, and
probably not without truth, of having employed
bribes to obtain the decisions which he sought from
the Papal Court. But it was, in his view, one thing
that gifts and largesses should be expended to expedite the progress of a suit which was in itself just
and salutary for the Church, and quite another thing
that the edicts of this final court of appeal should be
simply at the control of any one who chose to pay
highest for them, whether for or against the interests of the Church. Ancient custom had in a
measure excused the taking of large fees by those
connected with the Papal Court, and it was charitably presumed, doubtless, by men like Grosseteste,
that these money payments, though they might

quicken the progress of a suit, would not interfere with a really just settlement of it when it came to a hearing. It would not seem to him any thing shocking that he should pay heavily for obtaining an order such as that which he had lately obtained in the matter of the monasteries. But when he found that the Exempt Orders, when thus in danger of being made to perform the manifest duties which their tithe-property involved, could, by the payment of a larger sum, bring round the judge to their side, and defeat the efforts of a bishop anxious for the spiritual provision of his flock, it was then borne in on his mind that what should have been the fountain of justice was utterly corrupt and entirely venal. His moral sense revolted from dealing with such a polluted thing, and he cast it from him with indignation and loathing.

" The reason which took the Bishop of Lincoln across the seas was," says Matthew Paris, " patent to all. Though now an old man, he laboured without ceasing to bend more completely to his will those whom he had summoned to obey the Papal mandate, and who had appealed to the Apostolical See against his unheard of oppressions. For an appeal had been made by the Exempt Orders, the Templars, Hospitalers, and many others, who, by the intervention of a sum of money paid to the

Pope, prudently purchased for themselves immunity, following the advice of the heathen poet—'When the law is unjust, seek the help of the judge.' When this had become known to the bishop, after his great expenditure and labours all to no purpose, he came to the Pope overwhelmed with confusion and sorrow, and said to him, 'Holy father, I am struck with shame and confusion in this matter which I seek to further. I have trusted firmly in your letters and promises, but the hope which I had entertained turns out to be vain. Those whom I thought I had subdued now come off freely, to my utter confusion.'" To whom the Pope is said to have made answer with a stern and angry countenance, "Brother, what is this to thee? Thou hast freed thy soul; we have been pleased to extend our grace to them. 'Is thine eye evil because I am good?'" Then the bishop, heaving a deep sigh, said to himself, "'O money, money, how infinite is thy power! most of all in this Court of Rome[1]!' The Pope hearing him, and breaking out into a violent passion, exclaimed, 'O ye English, ye are

---

[1] Thus the Mediæval Satirist says,—
" Rome, in other graces frugal, not in avarice and greed,
  Has to spare for him who spares not, to the close is close indeed;
  Gold is still its golden idol, and *St. Mark* of saints the best,
  Of the altars where it worships, holy *chest* excels the rest."
                          Translated from Mapes' "Poems."

the most wretched of men.   Every one of you bites
and devours the rest, and strives to impoverish
them. Thou, too! how many religious persons who
are under thy control, thine own sheep, thine own
fellow-countrymen, and of thine own family, hast
thou laboured to ruin, that thou mightest seize
their goods for thine own tyranny and greed, to
make others, perhaps aliens, wealthy therewith.' "
The charge thus hurled at the bishop came naturally out of the corrupt conscience of the man who
made it. It was absurdly inapplicable to Grosseteste, who could not, in any instance, be shown to
have cared for wealth. But it was made by one
who was surrounded by sycophants who would ap-
plaud and lend force to even his most audacious
speeches. Thus we can easily lend credence to the
words of the historian that " the bishop, covered
with confusion, and exclaimed against by all as a
shameless fellow, had to retire[2]." Abashed and
disgraced, and doubtless feeling it all the more
bitterly, if it was the case that he himself had used
questionable means to obtain the decision in his
favour, Grosseteste retired from the presence of the
Pope. Yet he did not immediately quit Lyons.
There were other matters which he had to attend

[2] Matt. Paris, p. 773.

to besides that of the Exempt Orders of religious, and however bitterly he might feel, Grosseteste was not a man to neglect his duty[3]. He had to make a protest against the oppressive visitations of the metropolitan, which were spreading confusion through all the dioceses of England, and which Boniface was at that moment in Lyons to defend and uphold.

But especially he had to prepare himself for a more solemn and arduous duty. Convinced as he now was of the gross corruption of the Curia, and the Pope who presided over it, and feeling that all the evils and scandals of the Church were in fact upheld by them, his conscience obliged him, before leaving for ever this scene where such different parts ought to have been played, to deliver a final and energetic testimony against the foul blots which were allowed to deface the Church of God. The bishop had hitherto sought to combine intense devotion to the Papacy, on ecclesiastical grounds, with that ardent anxiety and care for souls which had been conspicuous in him throughout his whole career. To his devotion to the Papacy he had sacrificed much, but he still thought in doing so

---

[3] Matthew Paris says, with an unworthy sneer, "Ne nihil fecisse videretur aliis negotiis intendebat."

that he was promoting the main object of his life.
Now, however, these delusions were dispelled. He
found that in a necessary and fundamental part of
episcopal discipline he was thwarted and checked
simply because the wrong doers had money to
bribe the judge. He found that the highest officer
of the first Christian court, the Vicar of Christ on
earth, as he held him, scrupled not to tolerate the
robbery of tithes and endowments destined for support of those who minister in the things of God,
by establishments of indolent and selfish men—if
only these establishments had dexterously procured
an exemption from some former Pope, and were
wealthy enough to pay for its continuance. Moved
by these considerations, and desiring to free his
soul, the bishop wrote his famous sermon,
pamphlet, or protest, which, by a happy miscalcu-
lation as to its contents, he was able to get
delivered in the very presence of those whom it
principally touched, and which must indeed have
moved the hearts of those who heard it, hard and
callous though their hearts may have been. This
important sermon, so completely illustrating
Grosseteste's character and views, will be found
in an abbreviated form in the following chapter.

CHAPTER X.

GROSSETESTE DENOUNCING THE PAPAL COURT.

1250.

Bishop Grosseteste's Sermon on the abuses of the Court of Rome, and the Scandals prevalent in the Church; read before the Pope and Cardinals at Lyons.

A SERMON of Robert, Bishop of Lincoln, delivered before the Pope and Cardinals at the Council of Lyons[1] :—

In the year of our Lord 1250, on the third of the Ides of May, the venerable father Robert, Bishop of Lincoln, being in the presence of the lord Pope, Innocent III., and the Venerable Fathers the Cardinals, no one standing by his side save me, *Richard*[2], Archdeacon of Oxford; having first asked permission and awakened attention to

---

[1] Parts of this sermon are here translated literally. Other parts are abbreviated in the translation, and some parts are altogether omitted. Grosseteste's surplusage and redundancy of words would make an absolutely literal translation unreadable.

[2] This probably ought to be *Robert*, as Robert de Marisco was Archdeacon of Oxford at that time.

what was about to be put forth by him, handed that which here follows, firstly, to the lord Pope; secondly, in another copy, to the Lord William, Bishop of Sabina, and Cardinal; thirdly, in another copy, to the Lord Hugo, Presbyter, Cardinal of Saint Sabina; fourthly, to the Lord John, Cardinal-Deacon of St. Nicholas in the Tullian prison, saying that in each of these copies was contained that which he wished to put forth to them. Which writing was, in the hearing of the lord Pope and the Cardinals, almost without interruption, read through by the said John, Cardinal-Deacon, as follows :—

"Our Lord Jesus Christ, eternal Son of the eternal Father, out of the most secret bosom of the eternal Father descended into the womb of an humble and poor Virgin, being in the form of God, equal to the eternal Father, taking human flesh in her and from her, humbling Himself to the form of a servant. The Lord of power and the King of glory, with Whose glory heaven and earth are filled, was made of no reputation, despised, the least esteemed among men, a man of sorrow and acquainted with grief, looked upon as a leper, stricken of God and brought low, worn down in weakness by the Lord. He, upon the beauties of Whose face

angels desire to gaze, was made as One having no
form nor comeliness. He, upon Whom no suffering
or hurt could fall, was made full of grief; to Whose
grief both in soul for the sins and destruction of
the human race, and in body, especially on the
Cross, there is no other grief like. Zeal for the
salvation of souls, than which there is no sacrifice
greater nor more acceptable to God, led the Lord
of power and the King of glory to these things.
When about to leave the world and to enter into
His glory, from the same zeal and with the same
end, He sent His apostles (informed by His doctrine
and example, and as far as human weakness
allowed, made like unto Him and united to Him,
and made imitators of Him in all things) into all
the world, to preach the Gospel to every creature,
giving them power over all devils and to cure all
manner of disease. Who, going forth with the
other disciples, preaching every where, the Lord
working with them and confirming the word by
signs following, quickly filled the world with a
faith in Christ which was not dead, but living in
powers and operations. And because they could
not bear the burden of the pastoral office for the
whole world alone, nor for ever; like Moses, in
order to help them and continue the work, they

ordained and constituted fellow-labourers in the Gospel, pastors, men of power and fearing God, in whom the truth was; haters of covetousness, elders, not so much in years as in wisdom and virtue. This done, to encourage the first planters of the faith, they gladly and exultingly gave themselves up to the most cruel sufferings and to death, that they might be the martyrs and witnesses of Jesus Christ and of the truth of His doctrine. Those pastors who succeeded them, like them seeking not their own but those things which are of Jesus Christ, as far as human power enabled them, in holy deeds and the endurance of tribulations even to the shedding of blood, preserved the faith of Christ. And though all pastors in common are but one in the first Pastor Christ, and all represent Him and occupy His place, yet, by a special prerogative, those who preside in this most sacred See, the most holy Popes, are peculiarly the representatives and vicars of Christ; as the cardinals represent the apostles, and other pastors those first fathers. All of these ought incessantly to labour to bring about that which we pray for, viz., that the kingdom of God may come, and that the king may find guests at the marriage supper of His son. But alas! alas! alas! this faith meant to be spread widely about has been shut up in a very narrow compass. A great part of the world is occupied by unbelief and separated from Christ; of the part called Christian a great part has been severed from Christ by schism; of the remainder, heretical wickedness has taken away from Christ no small share, so that the Lord laments with mournful voice, saying, 'Woe is Me, I am made like one who gleans grapes in autumn, there is no bunch fit to eat; the fruit has perished out of the earth.' Now the cause of this trouble is evident. It is the want of those good pastors of whom I have spoken, and the multiplication of evil pastors, and the restraining of the pastoral power; for as these things were the means of spreading the religion of Christ throughout the world, so their opposites are the cause of unbelief, schism, heresy, and vice. Nor is this to be wondered at, for they do not preach Christ by their lives, but are dead, and so are the slayers of souls rather than the givers to them of life[3]. They are, by not preaching Christ, anti-Christs, and as Satan transformed into an angel of light. But, besides this, they add to their negligence every sort of vice, their pride is most open,

[3] At this point begins the passage quoted by Wycliffe in his Apology.—See Todd's "Wycliffe's Apol.," p. 54.

their cupidity and avarice abound, they follow greedily after gain. They are the robbers of widows and orphans, they pillage the covering of their flock and tear the flesh from their bones, they break even their bones in pieces. Moreover they are all most full of lust, fornicators, adulterers, incestuous, gluttonous, and, in a word, stained with every sort of crime and abomination[4]. Now, as the life of the pastors is the book of the laity, it is evident that such as these are the teachers of all errors and wickednesses. Thus, they are in truth teachers of heresy, as the word of action is stronger than the word of speech, and they are worse than the Sodomites of the body, in that they defile the soul.

"But what is the first cause and origin of this so great evil? Vehemently do I tremble and fear to speak it; but yet I dare not hold my peace, lest I should fall into that woe of the prophet, saying, 'Woe is me, because I have held my peace; because I am a man of unclean lips[5].'

"The cause, the fountain, the origin of all this, is this Court of Rome, not only in that it does not put to flight these evils, and purge away these

[4] Certainly a more terrible picture of the state of the clergy has never been drawn than this.

[5] Isaiah vi. 5.

abominations, when it alone has the power to do
so, and is pledged most fully to do so; but still
more, because by its dispensations, provisions, and
collations to the pastoral care it appoints before
the eyes of this sun, men such as I have described,
not pastors but destroyers of men; and, that it
may provide for the livelihood of some one person,
hands over to the jaws of the beasts of the field,
and to eternal death, many thousands of souls, for
the life of each one of which the Son of God was
willing to be condemned to a most shameful death.
It commits the care of the flock, in the midst of
ravening wolves, bears, and lions, to one who will
only take away the milk and the wool; who is
unable, ignorant, unwilling, or careless to lead out
the flock, to drive it into the pastures, and to bring
it back to the fold; who will not in the least expose
himself to danger to shield the flock from the lions,
bears, and wolves. Is not this to hand over the
flock to devouring and death; and is not he who
does this guilty of the death of the flock, even
though some of it by chance should escape death?
Moreover, he who does not hinder this when he
can, is involved in the same crime. This be far
from him who holds most directly of any one on
earth the office of saving souls, and stands most

prominently in the place of Him who says by the Prophet, 'I will give you pastors according to my heart, which shall feed you with knowledge and understanding[6].' The doings of this court are, as it were, a book, and an instruction to all who have the right of patronage in parish churches, to have regard to the claims of kindred and the flesh, or to the recompensing of favours, or to pleasing the powerful, by preferring such as these to the pastoral care, that they may enrich themselves, and thus destroy Christ's sheep. They are an instruction to them to despise things eternal and to seek, right or wrong, the things of this world, and to hold happiness to consist in these. The crime is greater in proportion as he who commits it is more highly placed, and the cause of evil is worse than its effect. Nor let any one say that this court acts thus for the common advantage of the Church. This common advantage was studied by those holy fathers who endured suffering on account of it,—it can never be advanced by that which is unlawful or evil. Woe to those who say let us do evil that good may come, whose damnation is just. Nor let any one say that such pastors as those of whom I have spoken

<hr>

[6] Jer. iii. 15.

save the flock by means of deputies, for among these deputies there are many hirelings, who, when they see the wolf coming, leave the sheep and flee, and the wolf catcheth and scattereth the sheep. The work of the pastoral care does not consist alone in administering the sacraments, saying the canonical hours, and celebrating masses (and even these offices are seldom performed by the mercenaries), but *in the teaching of the living truth*, in the awful condemnation of vice, and the severe punishment of it when necessary, and this but rarely can the mercenaries dare to do. It consists also in feeding the hungry, giving drink to the thirsty, covering the naked, receiving guests, visiting those sick and in prison, especially those who belong to the parish, who have a claim upon the endowments of their church. By the doing of these things is the people to be instructed in the holy duties of life. These duties cannot be performed by deputies and mercenaries, inasmuch as they scarce receive out of the goods of the Church enough to support their own lives, and if all that is intended to strengthen and aid the direction of souls be taken away from the office, how can it be properly carried on? This bad use of their office is greatly to be lamented in the case of secular incumbents, but then there is the hope, in their case, that some others may succeed of a better mind.   When, however, parish churches *are appropriated to religious houses*, these evils are made perpetual.   Oh, thing most prodigious and horrible, that thus should arise the chief and principal opposition to the Lord Christ and His work on earth !   Are not the words of the Prophet true of those who do this, being, as they are, for the most part, priests? ' The priests have violated My law, and have profaned Mine holy things : they have put no difference between the holy and profane, neither have they showed difference between the unclean and the clean, and have hid their eyes from My Sabbaths, and I am profaned among them[7].'

" Those who preside in this see are specially the representatives of Christ, therefore ought they specially to exhibit the works of Christ, and doing so, ought to be obeyed in all things as Jesus Christ.   But if any of them should put on the garment of favouritism, or of the flesh, or the world, or of any thing else besides Christ, and so from the love of this should command any thing opposed to the precepts and will of Christ, he that obeys him in matters of this sort manifestly sepa-

7 Ezek. xxii. 26.

rates himself from Christ and from His body, which is the Church, and from the Pope, as representative of Christ and true Pope; and should there be a general obedience paid to him in such matters, then there is a true and complete apostasy, and the revelation of the Son of Perdition is close at hand. God forbid that this most holy see and those who occupy it, should be the cause of a real apostasy. God forbid, also, that, inasmuch as there are some truly united to God and unwilling in any way to oppose His will, this see and its occupants, by commanding such as these to do that which is opposed to the will of Christ, should be the cause of an apparent apostasy or schism. Let them, therefore, neither enjoin any thing, nor do any thing which is discordant from the will of Christ; to Whom nothing is more abominable and odious than the destruction of souls, and therefore than the committing of them to those that are not pastors but destroyers, such as we have described. But the pastoral power which was given to the Apostles, and also to bishops the children of the Apostles, is at this day, especially in England, very much straightened and fettered. Firstly, by exemptions, which in the Church triumphant have no place. These exempt persons, so that—even if, when beyond the bounds of their monasteries, they commit fornication, adultery, or any other enormous and diabolical crime—they are free from the power of bishops and pastors. Pastors see their sheep murdered by ravening wolves, and yet, by the exempt privileges of these monks, are so fettered that they cannot call aloud to withdraw them. Pastors are so bound that when the wolves are actually attacking the flock, they cannot go forth to oppose them. When the Chief Shepherd, in that strict judgment, shall require at their hands the blood of the sheep thus slain before their eyes, what excuse will they be able to allege, save perchance the putting off the charge on those who grant these exemptions and privileges. Secondly, by the secular power, which does not permit inquiries into the sins of the lay folk to be conducted so as to arrive at the truth by putting the oath to other lay people. Thirdly, by the defences of appeals; for when a bishop, or any other pastor, strives to drive away from his people the demons of fornication, adultery, and other crimes, and to heal the maladies of vices, some of them, by the subtleties of lawyers, immediately utter an appeal to this see, and for defence of it to the archiepiscopal see[8], by the

[8] There are two sorts of appeal here mentioned, one the

defences of which see they are able, like brute beasts, to rot in the filth of their vicious pleasures at least for a year, and, as often happens, for ever. Fourthly, by appeals direct to the archiepiscopal see, in the court of which, causes of this sort are handled with all the subtleties and solemnities of the civil law, and the correction of vices is put off for a long period, perhaps entirely, and often the pastor is so wearied that he is tired of his life. Thus the zeal and diligence of pastors for healing the diseases of their people grows lukewarm and languishes. Not many physicians would fail to relax their cares if a patient himself repelled their medicines, and if some one else more powerful than they restrained them from obliging him to use the proper remedies. Should a bishop out of zeal for souls, repel or remove from the pastoral care such as these, who are useless, yea, worse than useless for this office, if they be men of the world and hold offices or dignities in the State, or are connected or intimate with those who hold them, straight-way will the bishop be calumniated in the matter of his own liberties and those of the Church, and

appeal to Rome, of which the archiepiscopal see was called to take charge—the other, the appeal to the archiepiscopal see direct.

be subjected to intolerable vexation; and even should the secular power be unfavourable to them, they will not desist from their legal quibbles until they have entirely overthrown the attempt of the bishop. Each art is best performed according to its own laws, and so the highest art, the providing for the salvation of souls, ought to be carried on by the laws which God has provided for it, namely, by the Gospels, which are to be the standards and measures of its right performance. Let, then, this holy see use its power to meet these evils which clearly endanger souls, and let it drive away by the eminence and plenitude of its power all such things, bringing into the world things altogether salutary and holy. For this is it established over nations and kingdoms, that it may destroy all evil and erroneous things, and cause all holy things to be firmly settled by being done continually and in love. But the clamour of the unbridled shamelessness of those who are of the family of this court, is multiplied with excessive vehemence, so that we may ask how can this court be said to preside well over its own household? And how shall it care for the Church of God, if it does not know how to govern its own household, or does not care to do so? Not to care for the morals of one's own family is to deny the faith. *Yet the family of this court has filled the world with lies,* has put to flight all modesty, has taken away all confidence in documents, and has lent all boldness to falsifying one's word. By disobeying the precept given to Peter, ' Put up thy sword into the sheath,' it invites upon it the woe denounced : ' All they that smite with the sword shall perish by the sword.' Abraham, Moses, and Samuel, the types and figures of this court, refused to receive gifts, and the Lord has commanded that judges should not receive presents which blind their eyes; yet the world sees with wonder that this most holy court receives gifts for the decision of causes. Moses and Samuel oppressed and afflicted no one; but the whole people and clergy of England murmur against this court for having conceded to the Lord of Canterbury the first-fruits of all the benefices in the province of Canterbury for a year, which were levied with the utmost violence and oppression, although the Church of Canterbury was sufficiently provided for the payment of its own debts[9]. Let no one ex-

---

[9] This is noteworthy. It will be remembered that Grosseteste himself had five years before assisted in carrying forward these exactions. He had doubtless been deceived as to the revenues of

cuse these things by saying that the days are evil, and the world full of mischief, and that, therefore, one must shut one's eyes to many things, and put up with many things for the general advantage of the Church; as though even the smallest evil were to be done to bring about even the greatest good. In proportion as the days are more evil ought we the more diligently to keep ourselves from all evil actions, and to cling to those things which are good. Where the battle presses most, there ought sloth and cowardice to be most carefully avoided, and the fight most boldly carried on. It is much to be feared, yea, rather it is certain, that the calamities under which this holy see is now labouring, and the absence from it of all good things, have been brought upon it by doing such evil things that good might come of them. Unless it corrects itself in these things without delay, quickly will it be utterly deprived of all good things, and when it shall say peace and safety, then shall sudden destruction come upon it, and it shall be subjected to the most terrible woes, which God the Father hath lamented by the mouth of His only-begotten Son, and of the dis-

the archbishopric and the justice of the claim. Now he sees more clearly.

ciple especially loved by Him, and by the mouth
of the Lawgiver, and all the holy prophets who
have been since the world began. These few things
with fear and trembling I hand in writing to your
Holy Fatherhood, being impelled by a vehement
dread of that woe which terrified Isaiah, and being
urged on by a desire to obtain the correction of
the evils which I have touched. Think it not,—
most humbly, earnestly, with anxious heart and
abundance of tears, I entreat you,—think it not, in
your paternal kindness, an act of presumption,
that, impelled by this fear and this earnest desire,
I, a grievous sinner, have ventured upon this ex-
hortation[1]."

[1] Brown, "Fasciculus rerum expetend. et fugiend.," ii. 250,
258.

CHAPTER XI.

GROSSETESTE'S RENEWED EFFORTS FOR REFORM.

1250—1252.

Adam de Marisco's congratulations to Grosseteste on his noble conduct—Grosseteste's return—His letter to the clergy of his diocese—Renewed efforts at reform—Strongly denounces the Romans intruded into English livings—Proceedings at Dunstable about Archbishop Boniface—Decision obtained from the Pope—Severe visitation of the monasteries—The Pope's letters empowering him to override exemptions of monasteries—Beneficed persons not in priests' orders succeed in withstanding his authority by help of the Pope—Case of Hurtold, the Burgundian, appointed to a living by the queen—Grosseteste successfully opposes the subsidy claimed from the Church by King Henry—The king's solemn engagement not relied upon by Grosseteste—He causes the violators of Magna Charta to be excommunicated.

THE news of Grosseteste's solemn and indignant protest against the evils which were pressing upon the Church, gave intense pleasure to his friends at home, and to none more than to Adam de Marisco, the zealous and talented Franciscan, the man completely after the bishop's own heart. He had longed earnestly to have accompanied the bishop, but the duties which he owed to his Order, and the demands on his time and services made by the king and queen, had hindered him. To him, therefore, Grosseteste at once communicated the important news of his protest, and we have the letter of Adam addressed to the bishop at Lyons in reply. He begins by remarking how terrible a thing it is to hear that even after such an exposure and so solemn a warning, no signs of change and reformation were visible. Was it, he says, to be an illustration of the text, " They did not hear him, because the Lord would slay them[1]." To Grosseteste, he says, be all honour as to one that had contended boldly for the truth, as did Elias, John Baptist, Paul, and Stephen; and though amazed at the wickedness which is abroad, he can take comfort in the thought, " If the Lord be for us, who can be against us[2]?" He is a mere mercenary who, in evil times, would desert the Lord's fold. He is rejoiced to hear that Grosseteste has no intention of this sort. There are grievous evils

1 1 Sam. ii. 25.   2 Rom. viii. 31.

P

in his diocese which need correction, and he prays that prudence and strength may be given him to perform this[3]. A little later, Adam writes again in a still more jubilant and exulting strain at the glorious work which Grosseteste had done, which could never have been accomplished save by " apostolical holiness, and prophetical inspiration." " O how wonderful, O how admirable, O how amiable, is the fruit of your labour, which for some short time at least breaks the power of those sins which cumber the world, and for all time lends encouragement and vigour to the defenders of the camp of the Lord." He eagerly desires to know when Grosseteste may be expected to return, that he may be prepared to greet fittingly this great champion of the Faith[4].

Although after the delivery of his protest Grosseteste's sojourn at Lyons could not have been very agreeable, he nevertheless remained some time longer there. His sermon was delivered on May 13, and his return to England is noted by Matthew Paris as having taken place about the Feast of St. Michael (1250)[5]. He returned, says

---

[3] Monumenta Franciscana, pp. 153, 157.
[4] Monumenta Franciscana, pp. 157-8.
[5] Matt. Paris, p. 802.

the chronicler, " sad and listless." The words are beyond measure expressive when applied to the vigorous and unhesitating character of the Bishop of Lincoln. He felt as though there were no work left for him to do, as though his mighty projects for cleansing and purifying the Church of God were all abortive and ruined. " And," continues Matthew Paris, " when he had come to his diocese, perceiving matter for confusion in the universal Church very threatening, he longed for himself to be free for contemplation, prayer, and study. Following then the example of Nicholas, Bishop of Durham, he divested himself of those worldly cares, in which he had been entangled all to no purpose, and handing over to Robert de Marisco, his official, all the business of the see which he was competent to do, he proposed to say farewell to the perishing world and to resign his bishopric. But fearing the robberies of the king, which were wont to empoverish vacant sees, and to intrude unworthy persons into them, with underhand compacts made, he suspended his secret designs and waited with anxiety, being unable to determine what to do in so great a confusion of the world[6]." The Lanercost Chronicle, which,

---

[6] Matt. Paris, p. 802.

though worthless as an historical authority, was written not far from the time of the bishop, and might possibly convey accurately his feelings and purposes at this important period of his life, also implies his intentions of resigning. " So great was the eloquence of this great man, that he found no equal in England in this respect; so great was his zeal for righteousness, that when called to the Roman court, in the presence of the Pope and all his brethren, in freedom of spirit and eloquence he preached publicly, and reproved the avaricious ways of the court, and would there and then have resigned his pastoral care, nor would have been willing, according to the bad customs, to offer any thing to the fathers of the court for taking it again,—whence those greedy ones called him the boastful Englishman[7]." The sentence here is obscure, but an intention or proposal to resign is certainly indicated. Yet it is extremely doubtful whether any such intention was entertained by the bishop. With regard to Matthew Paris, though he is very much to be relied upon for matters of fact, yet as to intentions he may have guessed, and guessed wrongly. Certainly with regard to intentions there is no authority so

7 Chron. de Lanercost, S.A. 1235.

good as the bishop himself, and his words to his friend, Adam de Marisco, seem to be incompatible with any purpose of resigning, nor in his letter written to his clergy immediately on his return, is there any such purpose to be traced. In this sad and solemn letter he declares himself touched with grief of heart, "at beholding evils so manifold, so grievous, so hideous, so foul, so heinous, so guilty, so wicked, so sacrilegious, every where existing in the people redeemed by the blood of Christ, and clinging to them by the neglect of those who should govern them, by the carelessness of the shepherds, and, (a matter rather for tears than for writing) by the most evil example, and contaminating mischief, every where spreading without shame. At beholding this I am altogether dissolved in despair, and I know not where to begin to provide a remedy for these things." . . "Behold, beloved, behold, in a day when ye think not, and at an hour when ye do not expect Him, our God cometh, and the eternal Lord who hath founded the ends of the earth is revealed. Behold, I say, He cometh, citing us all and each, by the voice of the archangel and the last trump to a general council, to the judgment of all flesh; about to make a visitation with His sword, which is hard so that none can bear it, which is great so that none can escape it, which is strong so that none can resist it. God is not mocked. I cry aloud that even now ye should awake and be watchful for the work ye have undertaken, that ye should redeem the time which has been lost, so shall ye find the judge about to come in some measure appeased. I know not how long I shall remain, or whether after a little while my Creator may take me away. I beseech you, with all the affections and the inmost bowels of my heart, that you, who for your office are held the children of God, may not be involved in ruin among the children of the world. Arise, beloved, arise, and watch for yourselves and your flocks ; feed them, as ye are bound, with the word of life ; feed them with example and the sacrament of life. I have been constrained to write this to you by the burden of my office which has been imposed upon me, and under which I groan with sorrow, because I cannot by my corporal presence fulfil that which I desired. In fine, recommend your-selves and your flock to the merciful Redeemer and the powerful Saviour of all souls. I leave this as my testament to you, that is to say, zeal for souls—zeal which, because it is lukewarm and slight in me, I pray you to increase by your prayers.

Let us all pray in common, that from the truth of the Gospel, from the love of our flock no human fear may ever tear us, but that the Lord would grant to us with all confidence to run speedily in the way of His commandments. To you, my archdeacons, and your officials, I give command that you publish these letters in your synods and chapters next to be held, and bring them to the knowledge of all rectors and vicars of what condition soever, that they may have no excuse and that I may escape the charge of silence[8]." The overpowering sense of responsibility and the tone of almost despair, which are apparent in this letter, are just what we should expect an ardent spirit like that of Grosseteste to give utterance to, after his experience of the tainted atmosphere of the Papal court. But despair and inaction could not long be acquiesced in by him. He quickly girded himself up to new and still more vigorous efforts to reform his clergy and to remove the obstacles which stood in the way of the efficiency of the Church. To quote Matthew Paris once more: "In those days (1251) the Bishop of Lincoln made a scrutiny and diligent inquisition and inquiry throughout his diocese, compelling the beneficed

<hr>

[8] Gross. Epist. cxxx.

clerks to observe continency, and not allowing
them to retain in their houses, as housekeepers, any
women of whom there could be suspicion. He
punished the transgressors by depriving them of
their benefices, and used his utmost endeavour to
cleanse his diocese from vice. Some he drew by
gentle entreaties, others he drove by solemn persuasion to enter the order and degree of priesthood.
Frequently also he preached to the people, compelling all the priests in the neighbourhood, under
fixed penalties, to be present to hear him[9]." The
course of the bishop's visitation speedly took him
to Dunstable, and here on the week before Lent
(1251)[1] there met him Fulk Basset, Bishop of
London, who had been the object of Archbishop
Boniface's most violent attacks in enforcing his
metropolitan visitation, as also the Bishops of
Salisbury and Norwich, and the proctors of other
bishops who were unable to attend personally.
After solemn deliberation on the claims of the
archbishop to exact his " procurations " throughout the whole Province, they came to the determination that these claims were to be strongly
resisted. They then drew up a document to which

[9] Matt. Paris, p. 826.
[1] Incorrectly dated 1250 in the Dunstable Annals, Ann.
Monast., iii. 181.

they set their seals, and "in good faith took a mutual engagement that with common help and counsel they would resist the archbishop." Each bishop undertook to move his clergy to contribute towards the expense of the suit. The Bishop of Lincoln was able to inform them from recent experience that money was an essential part of a suit before the Pope. They agreed on a rate of twopence for every mark of income, and appointed proctors, one for the bishop, and one for the clergy in each diocese, who were to go for them to the Pope, now at Perugia, and transact the necessary business of advancing their cause[2]. The archbishop, thoroughly alarmed at this calm and systematic opposition to his proceedings, hastened away also to the Pope to meet the proctors of the bishops, and to defend as best he could his malversations and oppressions. The Burton Annals furnish us with an account of the issue of the dispute, which must have been highly satisfactory to Grosseteste and those who had acted with him. It is true they had to pay, as they expected, somewhat highly for the decision in their favour, but the Annalist tells us "the lord Pope, for the sum of four thousand marks, ordained as is written below in the special

[2] Ann. de Dunstapliâ, Ann. Monast., iii. 181.

decretal then made." The substance of the decisions given was that, inasmuch as the Province of Canterbury has abundance of prelates who are diligent in attending to their duties, the parish churches of the several dioceses do not require a metropolitan visitation, and are therefore to be exempted and excused from procurations and from appearing before the archbishop, and that his censures of them are null and void. He is merely to be allowed to visit the officers of the diocese, and the heads of conventual establishments on one or two days, having for each day a procuration of four marks. At the same time the decree of the Lateran Council is quoted which limits the retinue of an archbishop visiting to forty or fifty horsemen; that of a bishop to twenty or thirty; that of an archdeacon to five or seven; that of a rural dean to two; and none of them are to take their hounds or hawks with them, or to indulge in sumptuous repasts[3]. These arrangements were to be carried out by Grosseteste, and the Bishops of London, and Bath and Wells[4], who

[3] Annal de Burton, Ann. Monast., i. 300—304.

[4] The Pope's letter is dated 1252, but the arrangement must have been made before that time, as Boniface was acting upon it previously to that. Dr. Hook speaks of him as returning to England at the end of 1252; but Matthew Paris says that he returned on the Feast of St. Barnabas, 1251.

are called conservators on this ground. Grosseteste thus to a certain extent atoned for the wrong he had done to the Church of England by encouraging Boniface in the exactions made at the beginning of his primacy.

Having settled the affair of the archbishop, Grosseteste turned with renewed vigour to his great work of visitation and correction. He had not as yet indeed any power over the Exempt Orders of religious, but there were many who had no privilege to plead against him, and these he determined not to spare. The vexations and opposition which he had undergone, his defeat at the Papal court, and the consequent exultation of those who dreaded his hammer-like blows, had doubtless not tended to smooth a temper naturally severe, and the account given by Matthew Paris of this visitation may have been in the main correct. There must, indeed, have been some most pressing cause to induce a man so holy as Grosseteste to use such extraordinary treatment of nuns, as the Chronicler ascribes to him; and we may well believe that if it had been indeed so, it must have appeared in other records of the time as a testimony against the bishop. As it is, we have only the assertion of Matthew Paris to establish it, and this must be taken with a remembrance of all that might move him as a monk, to give a prejudiced and exaggerated view of the bishop's conduct. This, then, is the account of Matthew Paris:—" In those days the Bishop of Lincoln made a visitation of those houses of religious which were established in his diocese; in which, if any one should repeat all the tyrannies which he exercised, he would be judged to be not severe only, but utterly rigid and without any feelings of humanity in him. For when, among other places, he came to Ramsey, accompanied by a body of seculars, he personally examined the beds of the monks in the dormitory, going round all, and turning every thing upside down, and if he chanced to find any thing shut up he demolished it, and dashed the caskets to pieces, and any cups which he found bound with rings or furnished with feet, he trode under foot and broke to fragments, which, if he had acted in a little more temperate manner, he might at any rate have given whole to the poor. And (that which is really too bad to write), coming to the houses of the nuns, he caused them to undergo a personal examination, that it might be discovered whether there were corruption among them. He added, also, horrible curses on

the heads of those who transgressed their statutes,
curses which he drew from the writings of Moses ;
at the same time also reciting the benedictions of
Moses on them who should keep their law." It is
difficult to know whether it is in irony or in
earnest that the Chronicler subjoins, " But all these
things he is believed to have done that he might
restrain those placed under him, and for whose
souls he was responsible, from sin [5]."

The especial object of the bishop at this moment
was to rescue from the grasp of the monasteries
sufficient maintenance for a priest to minister to
each congregation in his diocese. But this was considered by these ill-used religious as an intolerable
grievance. And when at length the Pope,—either
repenting his late rebuff administered to Grosseteste, which, no doubt, had received the condemnation of all good men,—or, it may be, failing to
receive from the Exempt Orders sufficient bribes to
induce him to continue his protection to them,—
sent to the bishop the long-desired power to enable
him to erect vicarages in churches held by monasteries of whatever order, we find the monkish
historian raising a dismal wail, as though some great
outrage were being done. "In the course of the same

<hr>

[5] Matt. Paris, p. 815.

year," writes Matthew Paris, " Robert, Bishop of Lincoln, *that he might cripple the revenues of the religious* and increase the shares of the vicars, obtained from the Apostolical See a direction of this sort which he had before been waiting for :— ' Innocent, bishop, &c., to the venerable Bishop of Lincoln.   Whereas, we have been informed, that in your city and diocese certain religious persons and others who live in colleges obtain parochial churches to their own use, in which the allowances for vicars are either none or too slender, we, therefore, by our Apostolical letters command you, our brother, that in these churches you do institute, out of the rents of the churches, vicarages, where there are none, and where those already instituted are too slender, that you do augment them as from us, as you shall see it expedient, according to the custom of your country and in the sight of God.   *And it shall not hinder you if the aforesaid religious persons be exempt, or otherwise fortified by Apostolical privileges or indulgences,* by which it might be possible that this should be stopped or delayed, and concerning which there should be in these presents a special mention made; and you are permitted to coerce those who oppose you by ecclesiastical censures, without right of appeal.'   The aforesaid bishop (more, as is said, and appears to be the case, *out of hatred of the religious, than of love and care for the vicars*) by the authority of this mandate, inflicted upon many religious bodies injuries and oppressions[6]." That it should be held and asserted to be an " injury and oppression " to cause the monasteries to make some provision for the service of the Church, out of the revenues of the Church, and that the attempt of the bishop to do this should be branded as a mere act of hatred towards the religious bodies, by so exceptionally good a specimen of a monk as Matthew Paris, proves most clearly how thoroughly the evil system had taken root and become accepted, and how arduous was the task of Grosseteste in striving to break through it.

Cheered as he doubtless was by the obtaining this long-desired power to deal with the crying evil of monastic appropriations, Grosseteste yet had to suffer annoyance and disappointment at this time in another matter wherein the Pope was concerned. In a passage, quoted from Matthew Paris above, it was said that the Bishop of Lincoln used every means to make those who held benefices enter the order of priesthood. One would hardly

[6] Matt. Paris, p. 860.

suppose it possible to find that this so reasonable
a requirement could have met with any serious opposition. Yet so it was. The opposition, indeed,
was not only determined, but also successful, and
nothing perhaps could give us a worse picture of
the Church at that time than the record of this
transaction as found in Matthew Paris. The clerks
who clubbed together to evade their solemn obligations, and the Pope, who, for a bribe, permitted
this gross abuse, stand equally condemned. "At
that time, many beneficed persons in the diocese
of Lincoln having been efficaciously admonished
by the bishop to proceed to the grade of priesthood, whether they desired it or not, refusing to
submit themselves to the yoke of the Lord, took
measures as follows :—By common agreement they
collected a contribution among themselves, and
getting together a considerable sum, they sent it
to the Roman court; and the money being distributed according to the Pope's direction, by
means of that which, in that court is of chief
strength, they resisted the episcopal mandate, and
obtained licence to continue to teach for a certain
number of years without the priesthood. And
thus, with the appearance of honesty, they withdrew their necks from under the yoke of the Lord

with fox-like cunning[7]." The indignation at seeing ecclesiastical revenues treated as mere secular property, without involving any pastoral responsibilities, was destined to pursue Grosseteste throughout his whole career. The king, who, though in outward acts of observance more religious than his father, was yet as eager as John, whenever he safely could, to lay sacrilegious hands on church goods, encouraged by his example this grievous scandal. Grosseteste had good cause to fear his "rapines." Either he kept churches in his gift vacant that he might receive the revenues, or he set up suddenly some claim to lands held by a church, or he bestowed benefices on courtiers for some corrupt consideration. In giving his patronage, he had utter disregard for the rights of others as he had shown in the case of the prebend of Thame, and on numberless other occasions. At this time a case happened which brought Grosseteste into strong collision with him. Richard de Thiony, a noble Angevin, who is said to have got possession of many church revenues in France, England, and Scotland, having died, among his other benefices the living of Flamstead fell vacant. The queen considered that the patronage belonged to

[7] Matt. Paris, p. 833.

Q

her, as she was legal guardian of his nephew, Ralph,
to whom the advowson of the church belonged.
She appointed, therefore, a clerk to the living,
which was a very valuable one[8]. The king hearing of this, broke out into a violent passion against
the insolence and pride of women, and appointed
a favourite of his own, one Hurtold, a Burgundian.
Hurtold got possession, and ejected the queen's
nominee. The queen then bethought herself of her
friend, Bishop Grosseteste, and the bishop came
speedily to the rescue. Glad, no doubt, to have
the opportunity of testifying his displeasure against
Henry's tyrannical doings in church matters, he
excommunicated Hurtold, and interdicted the
church until its lawful rector could obtain possession[9]. The Bishop of Lincoln was indeed a for-
midable antagonist for Henry to grapple with.
He knew well the character of that false and timid
prince, and he did not scruple to act on his knowledge of it. Both in matters of Church and State
Henry constantly found him standing in opposition
to him, and wielding a power greater than his
own.

[8] Worth one hundred marks, according to Matthew Paris: a
very large sum for a benefice in those days. Eleven or twelve
marks is a usual value.

[9] Matt. Paris, p. 839.

At the Parliament held October 13, 1252, the king produced the Papal mandate giving him for three years an entire tenth of the revenues of the Church of England, which was to be estimated not according to the old computation of the value of churches, but by a new computation to be made by the king's officers. "With vulpine craft," says Matthew Paris, "the king's officers, assuming the consent of the bishops, explained to them the way in which the subsidy was to be paid. Which, when the Bishop of Lincoln heard, struck with amazement at these words so full of venom, and skilfully drugged to work the ruin of the Church, he answered in great wrath, 'O, by Our Lady, what is this? We are going somewhat too fast. Do ye suppose that we have consented to this cursed contribution? That be far from us thus to bow the knee to Baal.' To whom the elect of Winchester said, 'Father, how shall we resist the will both of Pope and king? One drives, the other draws. The French have agreed to a like contribution. They are stronger than we are, and more ready to resist.' To him replied the Bishop of Lincoln, 'For that very reason ought we to resist. For two acts may create a custom. Besides, clear enough is it what has been brought about by this tyrannical extortion of the French king.   Let neither the king nor us incur the heavy wrath of God.   For myself, I say it openly, I will not consent to this unjust contribution.'   The bishops, encouraged by this bold lead, immediately agreed. Then Grosseteste added, 'We will, however, put it to our lord the king, that for the good of his soul he should curb such rashness.'   The king on hearing this burst into an ungovernable fury; but afterwards, pressed by his necessities, he tried the effect of soft words."   In the answer of the bishops we trace very plainly the hand of Grosseteste, although the words are not directly assigned to him by the historian.   "We believe," they say, "that if our lord the Pope had known with how many oppressions and unjust exactions the English Church is weighed down, he would never have made this grant to the king, and that if we informed him of them he would recall it.   For the king at one time by extending his forests, at another by his itinerant justices, at another by the invention of new pleas, at another by some other mode, is pauperizing his kingdom; and if this be ruined, the Church must needs be ruined also.   What shall we say of the prelates whom he thrusts into noble churches? What extortions have not been practised by his

Archbishop Boniface, enough to cripple the whole Church of England. The king is reducing this realm of England, which once flowed with honey and all abundance, to a desert. Yet will we endeavour once more to satisfy him, if he will solemnly undertake to carry out the Charter, and give an undertaking that the English Church shall never again be subject to such an impost. The money, however, must be carefully applied to the purpose of the crusade for which it is sought[1]." As this was really the last thing the king intended, again he raged and stormed, but neither menaces nor soft speeches could allure the prelates, among whom Grosseteste was the ruling spirit, to yield to his demands.

With what feelings the king regarded the great Bishop of Lincoln who checked him in his patronage, thwarted him in his money schemes, and did not shrink from telling him the plainest truths in the plainest language, may be easily surmised.

At that famous scene which was exhibited at the Parliament held the following year, when the king, on the faith of the most solemn engage-

---

[1] Matt. Paris, pp. 849-851. The pretence of seeking the subsidy was a pilgrimage to the Holy Land.

ments, at length received a subsidy, and the awful excommunication was pronounced against all who should violate Magna Charta, Grosseteste bore a prominent part. The feeble king, who had readily made all promises, shrank from being the bearer of a candle in the excommunication scene, on the ground that he was not a priest. Doubtless Grosseteste, either from this hesitation, or from Henry's unhappy antecedents, divined the speedy falsification of the solemn promises then made, for says Matthew Paris, "The Bishop of Lincoln forecasting in his heart, and fearing lest the king should start back from his engagements, caused on his return to his see a solemn excommunication to be pronounced in every parish in his diocese, which for their great number can scarce be reckoned, against all breakers of these charters, and especially if they were priests,—a sentence which made the ears of the hearers to tingle, and their hearts to tremble not a little [2]."

[2] Matt. Paris, p. 867.

CHAPTER XII.

GROSSETESTE IN OPPOSITION TO THE POPE.

Sketch of the intrusion of foreigners into English benefices—The riots in 1231—Sir Robert de Twenge and the "Levythiel"—Grosseteste at first opposed to these views—He supports Martin, the Pope's tax-gatherer—Vigorous measures of the nobles against Martin—Grosseteste turns round in his views and refuses to admit an Italian—He is suspended by the Pope—Causes a calculation to be made of the income of foreigners beneficed in England—Pope's appointment of Frederick di Lavagna—Grosseteste refuses to institute him—His letter to the Pope—Various accounts of its effect—Grosseteste's appeal to the people of England.

WE now come to the final cause of quarrel between Bishop Grosseteste and the Pope, which arose from the intrusion of the Pope's nephew into a benefice in the diocese of Lincoln. But before we speak of this particular instance of Papal oppression, it will be well to take a glance backward, and to trace the beginning and growth of this custom of saddling

foreigners on English benefices. The base cession
of the kingdom made by John to the Pope, the
tutelage exercised by the Pope over Henry III. in his
earlier years, the growth of the legatine authority
in England, all encouraged the occupier of the
chair of St. Peter in the thirteenth century to treat
this country as a fief of the see of Rome, and to
dispose of its ecclesiastical revenues just as it
pleased him. "Is not the King of England my
vassal?" exclaimed the impetuous Innocent IV. at
Lyons. In this view the Pope was supported by
many of the English bishops, who thought that
they could gain more power and influence by adhering to him than by adhering to the popular
side. As to Henry, he was ever vacillating, at one
time conceding every thing to the Pope, at another
uttering furious protests, that through the Pope's
intrusion of foreigners, the " laws were broken, the
poor were cheated of their maintenance, the word
of God was not preached, churches were not cared
for, souls were neglected, no services were held in
churches, but even the walls and roofs were fallen
to decay and torn in pieces[1]." However, as the
king himself was as great an offender in this matter
as even the Pope, his protests could not carry much

[1] Matt. Paris, p. 699.

weight. We are indebted to the laity for the first effectual stand made against the gross abuse of foreign incumbents. About the year 1231 the grievance of the Papal intrusions seems to have come to a head. At that time mysterious letters began to be handed about to the various bishops and chapters, which ran in the following form:—' To such a Bishop, and such a Chapter :—The general company[2] of those who would rather die than be ruined by the Romans, sends greeting. You know well how the Romans and their legates have hitherto treated us and other ecclesiastical persons of England. They give the benefices of the kingdom to their people, just as they please, to the intolerable prejudice aud injury of you and all other persons in the kingdom. They fulminate sentences of suspension against you and the other patrons of livings to hinder you from conferring benefices on any one in the kingdom, until five Romans (who are not even named, but described thus, as the son of Rumfredus or the son of such and such an one) are provided for in the diocese, and each one with not less than a hundred pounds. They inflict also other injuries in great number, both upon laymen and the nobles of the land, in the matter of their

[2] Universitas.

advowsons, and their alms, given by them and their predecessors for the support of the poor of the kingdom, as well also as upon clerks and other religious persons, in their property and benefices. And, not contented with these things, they strive to take away altogether from the clerks of the kingdom the benefices which they hold, in order to confer them upon the Romans, not according to what is fitting, but according to their own will and pleasure, intending to fulfil in their case the prophecy, 'They spoiled the Egyptians that they might enrich the Hebrews;' multiplying the nation but not increasing the joy, heaping thus upon us and upon you grief upon grief, so that it seems better for us to die than to live under such oppressions. . . Wherefore, by common consent, we have chosen, although after long delay, to resist rather than any longer to submit to their intolerable oppressions, or to be subjected to even greater slavery. On these grounds we charge you and earnestly bid you that, when we use our endeavours to snatch the Church, the king, and the kingdom from so heavy a yoke of slavery, in the matter of those who interpose themselves for the Romans or their rents, that you should not on your part presume to interfere; giving you to understand that, if (which God forbid) you transgress this command, your property will be exposed to fire, and the penalty which the Romans will incur in their persons ye will in your possessions without doubt incur." Another letter was also addressed by the same secret society to those who held the churches or glebes of the Romans at farm, bidding them not to pay over the monies which were due from them to the foreign incumbents, but to keep them in hand until they were demanded by the proctors of the society.

These letters were despatched in every direction through the country by the messengers and agents of the secret society, sealed with a device representing two swords, and between the swords the legend " Behold, here are two swords[3]." The operations of the conspirators were not long confined to letters and menaces. One Cincio, a Roman clerk, Canon of St. Paul's, was seized not far from St. Alban's and carried off by some men in masks, and at Christmas the full barns of a Roman ecclesiastic

---

[3] Matt. Paris, p. 371. Dr. Pegge is quite in error in saying that these missives purported to come from the King's Council. The heading describes them as emanating from the general company of those who were affected by the unjust proceedings of the Romans; and the words "we have chosen of our common counsel" merely signify the joint determination of the body.

at Dingham were captured and plundered. The
sheriff of the county was called upon by the Proctor
of the Romans, and sent his officers to the spot,
but the masked conspirators showed them some
forged letters, pretending to be from the king, to
authorize their proceedings, and the sheriff's officers
were easily persuaded to leave them undisturbed.
The corn was brought out and sold at cheap rates
to the poor, and the movement thus taking the
sure way to obtain popularity, went on increasing
and spreading. All over England mysterious bands
suddenly appeared wearing masks, and ruthlessly
seizing on all property belonging to a foreign clerk.
This was always distributed to the poor, who rushed
eagerly to share in the unaccustomed spoil, even
the money captured being freely thrown among
them. The bold leader of these attacks gave his
orders in the name of William the *Witherer*[4], and
the men who followed him were known by the
name of *Lewythiel.* The real name of the patriotic
chief was Robert de Twenge, a knight of good
lineage, and of a fair estate in the north, who had
himself suffered a special hardship in having a
living in his gift seized twice consecutively for a

[4] "To *wither* is now used in the North for to throw about
hastily or in passion."—Pegge.

Roman[5]. As the Pope, on hearing of the general spoiling of his friends, and how they lay lurking in the monasteries in fear of their lives, began at once to thunder his excommunications, the king was forced to take up the matter, and a very large number of the chief persons in the land were found to be concerned in it. As for Sir Robert de Twenge, he did not care to conceal himself, but came forward, and openly avowed his share in the business, declaring his deadly hatred against Roman spoilers of the Church, and setting forth his own grievance in the matter of the church of Lytham[6]. His bold bearing and manifestly just cause not only saved him from molestation, but led the king and nobles to advise him to go in person to the Pope and state his grievance, and urge his claim. This Sir Robert readily undertook to do. He was fortified by letters from the king, and he also bore from some of the principal nobles a bold and telling missive. In this they declare that the ship of their liberties is fast sinking, and that they are constrained to awaken him who slumbers in the ship of Peter, lest all jus-

[5] It was specially covenanted in the Provisions that there should not be two foreign incumbencies consecutively, but this was often disregarded.

[6] On the sea coast of Lancashire, now well known as a bathing-place.

tice and right should perish. They had undoubted rights of presentation to churches, yet by the Pope's connivance these were taken from them, and one alien after another was thrust into their churches. This was the case with Robert de Twenge, who, at the death of a certain Italian rector, of his church at Lytham, presented a fitting clerk, who was refused by the Archbishop of York because of the Pope's command that benefices should be kept for the Romans. This was an intolerable injustice, inasmuch as the right of advowson was part of the feudal estate, for which they paid military service to the king, and they were therefore bound to call upon him to redress their wrongs. Before these claims so boldly urged, Pope Gregory appears to have retreated. It has, however, been ever the policy of Rome to affect justice in word and writing, which in act is often put aside. Sir Robert de Twenge and the nobles at his back obtained a conciliatory epistle, which said that it was far from the Pope's wish to take away the rights of presentation enjoyed by the laity in England; and the legate was instructed at once to see to the admission of his presentee to the rectory of Lytham. At this the monkish historian is seized with fury. "It may well be seen," he says, "what justice, reverence, and piety there were remaining. Only against ecclesiastical persons and unwarlike religious are plundering and spoiling of their goods to be allowed. O Church of Rome, ever greedily gaping, ever unsatisfied[7]." The same Pope who, in this year (1239) professed himself as entirely opposed to invading the rights of patrons, in the very next year (1240) made the iniquitous arrangement with the Roman citizens that they should have the power of distributing at their will the chief vacant benefices in England to their relatives, " especially those of religious bodies." It has been already mentioned that the Archbishop of Canterbury, the Bishops of Lincoln and Salisbury were specially charged with carrying out this "provision," and that there is good reason to believe that Grosseteste did not, as much as was fitting, support Archbishop Edmund in his resistance,—a resistance which at length quite overwhelmed him and led him to resign. Grosseteste, indeed, enjoyed a special privilege as regards these Papal provisions, namely, that he was not bound to institute a Roman unless the actual person were duly nominated. This, however, did not affect the principle of the matter. Could the Bishop of Lincoln, as one anxious for

<hr>

[7] Matt. Paris, pp. 513-14.

the souls of his people, institute a foreigner who had no intention of residing or labouring for the good of souls to a benefice in his diocese?   Unquestionably, during the earlier period of his episcopate, Grosseteste held that he could, and his distinct assent to the Pope's inordinate encroachments in the first instance gives an overpowering force to the attitude which he afterwards assumed. This change of view and position in the case of the bishop has been usually left out of sight by all writers of Church history, but it is surely of the utmost significance and importance.

It is evident that Grosseteste, with the view which he then held, could not have sympathized with Sir Robert de Twenge and his patriotic attempts, but must have considered the *Lewythiel* as grievously sacrilegious offenders, and have defended the claim of the Pope.   And so it was also later on when the new Pope, Innocent IV., following the steps of his predecessor, sent his agent Martin to exact money from the English Church, and to seize for foreigners the best benefices that should fall vacant. Matthew Paris mentions the audacious and barefaced extortions and assumptions of this man, with fitting indignation[8], but not

8 Matt. Paris, pp. 613, 641.

so Grosseteste. It seems that some of Martin's proceedings in the diocese of Lincoln had excited a tumult against him and his men, and he had referred to the bishop to ask his advice how he was to avenge himself. Grosseteste in reply declares himself desirous to serve the lord Pope and him; he doubts not their both having a single eye to the great end of the ministry—the salvation of souls; he advises him to excommunicate those who had resisted his men, but he puts in a word for the Prior of Spalding, whose right of appointing to the vicarage of that town had been claimed by Martin. "The place," says the bishop, "is large and requires a vicar constantly resident, and the lord Pope may easily provide for those whom he shall please to provide for in rectories which have not so large a cure. You may reserve some church in the patronage of the said prior, while you allow him to present to Spalding [9]." Very different from this were the answers given to Martin's demand by the general assembly of the nobles and prelates held at London to which he addressed requisitions for help for the Pope. In temperate language they decline to comply with his requests, alleging the injustice of the demand and the want of resources in the

9 Gross, Epist. cvi.

country, even if the claim were just, to satisfy it.
But Master Martin was destined to experience a
still more vigorous rebuff from the people and the
nobles of England. He had gone on in spite of
refusals, seizing by underhand means on benefices
and ecclesiastical rents, selling exemptions and
raising money by all sorts of practices. At length
the patience of the chief men of the land was ex-
hausted. They met at Luton and Dunstable under
pretence of a tournament, and having agreed to
decisive action, they despatched one of their number to bid Martin leave the kingdom within three
days if he valued his life. The Pope's agent at
once went for protection to the king; but Henry,
who was thoroughly disgusted with exactions in
which he had no profitable share, answered him
with a furious oath. Martin, in abject terror, was
only now desirous to escape with safety. He was
despatched to the sea under an escort, and Matthew
Paris relates with great glee his miserable terrors
and apprehensions of personal violence. "Then,"
said he, "did the Italians, fattened with the rich
revenues which they had got in England, suddenly
disappear and hide themselves[1]." To follow up
this vigorous proceeding the nobles of England

[1] Matt. Paris, p. 660.

despatched to the Pope, now holding his council at
Lyons, their complaint against the abuses perpetrated. They say that " their predecessors had
founded monasteries, and had endowed them with
goods and with the rights of patronage of churches,
that fitting clerks might be appointed to serve the
churches, and that the spiritual interests of the
land might be attended to. But now these churches
are seized on for Italians (of whom there is an infinite number beneficed in the country) who care
not for the flock, but carry off the rents into a
foreign land. Meantime the clergy of the country
are reduced to poverty and beggary. Master
Martin had lately been in the land with a power
never heard of before, seizing and conferring benefices just as he pleased, and exercising other extortions. Wherefore they, the nobles and whole
estate of England called upon the Pope for redress[2]."
But the Pope answered not. Probably he knew
that the less said on such an odious subject the
better. It has been already stated that at the
conclusion of the Council of Lyons the Pope organized another scheme for the plunder of the
English Church, and that in carrying out this,
Grosseteste acted as his agent, so that up to this

[2] Matt. Paris, pp. 666-89.

R 2

point (1246), in spite of his tender care for souls and the gross abuse of the foreign incumbents, the Bishop of Lincoln could not be brought to break away in revolt from that Papal system which he so earnestly cherished. But the time at length came when his views altogether changed. The scandal became so crying and grievous that no devotion to the Papal See could induce him to tolerate it longer. It is in the year following this that we have the account of Grosseteste's severe rebuff addressed to the two Minorite friars, who were attempting to collect for the Pope, which has already been quoted [3].

A little farther on Matthew Paris says of him, " Those rascal Romans who had the Pope's precept for obtaining a ' provision,' he hated like the poison of a serpent. He was wont to say, that if he should commit the charge of souls to them, he should be acting like Satan [4]. Wherefore he often threw down with contempt the letters sealed with the Papal Bulls and openly refused to listen to such commands."

His decided attitude of vigour and energy soon embroiled him with the Pope. " Innocent," says Dr. Pegge, " persisting in his old courses, notwith-

---

[3] Matt. Paris, p. 826.   [4] Sathanizaret.

standing all the fair promises and assurances that he had given to the contrary, commanded the bishop to admit an Italian, entirely ignorant of the English language, to a rich benefice in his diocese; but he, refusing to comply, was suspended for it in the Lent following." If this were indeed so, it does not seem to have troubled the bishop very much. By this time he had fully made up his mind to disregard altogether the Papal authority. He who could inflict so ruthlessly evils of such magnitude upon the Church, was not to be heard, when he interfered to censure a bishop acting according to his conscience in the discharge of his office. Thus at the grand ceremonial at Hales (November, 1251), Grosseteste is found bearing a principal part, and singing Mass at the high altar[5]. But neither pompous ceremonials, nor the busy and multitudinous labours to which he was at this time exposed, could divert the attention of Grosseteste from the monster grievance of the Church,

[5] The Earl of Cornwall had erected a magnificent monastery and church at Hales in fulfilment of a vow which he had made when in peril of shipwreck. The cost of the whole work was 10,000 marks. At the dedication were present the king and queen, and almost all the nobles and prelates of England. More than 300 knights were entertained, and a vast number of "religious." Thirteen bishops sang mass, and Grosseteste officiated at the principal altar.—Matt. Paris, p. 827.

which he had at length fully apprehended. "To such a pitch had the avarice of the Romans been allowed to grow," says Matthew Paris, "and such a point had it reached, that the Bishop of Lincoln being struck with amazement at it, caused his clerks carefully to reckon and estimate all the revenues of foreigners in England, and it was discovered and found for truth, that the present Pope, viz., Innocent IV., had pauperized the whole Church more than all his predecessors from the time of the primitive Papacy. The revenue of the alien clerks whom he had planted in England, and whom the Roman Church had enriched, amounted to more than 70,000 marks. The king's revenue could not be reckoned at more than a third part of this sum[6]." Hardly had this portentous calculation been completed, when the bishop became aware that there had arrived in England a letter from Pope Innocent, which, for its unblushing audacity, seemed to throw all other missives of the same sort into the shade. It was addressed to the "Archdeacon of Canterbury, and Master Innocent, our writer, sojourning in England," and ran thus:—
" Forasmuch as our beloved son, William, Cardinal of St. Eustace, has canonically conferred at our

<hr>

[6] Matt. Paris, p. 859.

special command, a canonry of Lincoln on our beloved son, Frederick de Lavagna, clerk, our
nephew, and by his ring has corporally invested him in the same, so that from that time
forward he became a Canon of Lincoln, and had
the full name and right of a canon and a
title to any prebend[7] which should become vacant
after the Bishop of Lincoln should have been informed by these letters as to receiving and providing for him in the same church, or which he
shall have reserved according to the apostolical
donation to be conferred upon its vacancy—Now
we decree void and vain any claim that has been
made on such a prebend by any one, and against
those who oppose and rebel we promulgate the
sentence of excommunication, as in the letters of
the same cardinal is more fully contained. And
moved by the prayers of the said Frederick, we
ratify and approve that which was done by the
said cardinal, and by our apostolical authority confirm it. Wherefore, by our apostolical writings we
command your discretion that you do induct the
said Frederick, or his proctor, into corporal pos-

---

[7] It should be remembered that *prebend* is the name of the
office or benefice; canon or prebendary the name of him who
holds it.

session of the said canonry and prebend, by your authority, and that you do defend him when inducted, restraining his opposers by ecclesiastical censures without appeal, without taking heed of any customs or statutes, oaths or confirmations of the Apostolical See, or any other security; or that the said Frederick is not present to make oath to observe the customs of the Church; or that the said bishop or chapter, either jointly or singly, have indulgences from the said see against being compelled to receive or provide for any one; or that there be any one else in their church thus exempt; or that the power of inflicting interdict, suspension, or excommunication, be taken away by any letters apostolic, which have been obtained or may be obtained, even if the whole tenor of such indulgences, word for word, be inserted in such letters, or [be inserted] in any other indulgences conceded to any persons, dignity, or place, by the See Apostolic, under any form of words, or to be conceded hereafter, by which the effect of these presents might in any way be hindered or deferred. Such (indulgences) we will of our certain knowledge, as far as relates to the provision made and to be made for the said Frederick in the Church of Lincoln, to be altogether without force.   But if any oppose the said Frederick, or his proctor, in any of the premises, these ye shall take care to have cited peremptorily to appear before us within the space of two months, to answer to the said Frederick in the premises, without regard to the privileges or indulgences granted by the said see to the persons of the kingdom of England generally, or to any person, dignity, or place specially, viz., that they may not, by letters Apostolic, be summoned to trial beyond sea, or beyond the limits of their city or diocese; which privilege and indulgence we do not allow to such persons, the constitution *de duabus dictis,* published in a General Council, notwithstanding. The day and form of citation you are to intimate to us by your letters. But if both of you are unable to be present to perform these things, let one of you do so. Given at Perugia, 7 Kal. February, in the tenth year of our Pontificate." This letter is worth reproducing literally, as probably no better specimen could be found of a composition, which <u>studiously</u>, and with elaborate phraseology, sets itself to override all considerations of justice and equity, all previous solemn engagements and promises, in order to inflict a gross outrage and scandal upon the Church.

In reply to this document, Bishop Grosseteste

at once addressed to those who had received it from
the Pope, and who doubtless had communicated it
to him, the following :—" I understand that you
have received a letter from the lord Pope to the
following effect. (Then follows the letter.) It is
well known to your wisdom that I am ready to
obey Apostolical commands with filial affection, and
all devotion and reverence ; but to those things
which are opposed to Apostolical commands, I,
being zealous for the honour of my parent, am
opposed, for by the divine direction I am equally
bound to both of these things. For Apostolical
commands are not, and cannot be any other than
those which are agreeable to the doctrine of the
Apostles, and to Jesus Christ Himself, the Master
and Lord of the Apostles, Whose figure and re-
presentation is specially borne by the lord Pope
in the ecclesiastical hierarchy. For our Lord Jesus
Christ Himself says, ' He who is not with Me is
against Me,' but against Him the most divine
sanctity of the Apostolical See, neither is nor can be.
The letter above mentioned is not in its tenor
agreeable to Apostolical holiness, but is very alien
from it and altogether discordant. In the first
place in this letter, and in others like it spread
widely abroad, the ' notwithstandings ' which are

heaped up in such vast quantity, being not drawn from any necessity of observing the law of nature, produce a wide deluge of fickleness, audacity, and shameless insolence of lying and deceiving, a distrust in believing or giving faith to any body, and all the vices which follow from these things, which are innumerable, disturbing and confusing the purity of the Christian religion, and the quiet of social intercourse among men. Secondly, since the sin of Lucifer, with which that of Anti-Christ, the Son of Perdition, in the latter times will be the same, ' whom the Lord Jesus shall destroy with the breath of His mouth,' there neither is nor can be any sort of sin so adverse and contrary to the doctrine of the Apostles and the Gospel, and to the Lord Jesus Christ Himself; so hateful, detestable and abominable, and to the human race so destructive, as to kill, and destroy, by robbing them of the pastoral office and ministry, those souls meant to be quickened and saved by the office and ministry of the pastoral care. And this sin, Holy Scripture clearly shows is committed by those who, having power over the pastoral care, provide for their own carnal and temporal desires and necessities from the milk and wool of the sheep of Christ, and do not administer

the fitting duties of the pastoral office to work the
eternal salvation of the sheep of Christ. For the
non-administration of pastoral offices is by the
testimony of Scripture, the slaying and destruction
of the sheep. But that these two sorts of sins,
although in unequal degree, are the worst of sins,
and infinitely surpass all other sorts of sin, is clear
from this, that they are, though unequally and
dissimilarly, the direct contrary to the two
best things; and that thing is the worst which is
contrary to the best. One of these (that of Anti-
Christ) is the vilifying of the Deity itself, which
is super-essentially and supernaturally the best, but
the other is the destruction of that which is in the
form of God, and the best of God's works essentially and naturally, because it participates in the
gracious gift of the divine Spirit. And, inasmuch
as in good things the cause of good is better than
the effect, so in evil things the cause of evil is also
worse than the effect. Clearly, therefore, those
who introduce into the Church of God such slayers
of the divine image and handiwork in the sheep of
Christ, are worse than the murderers themselves,
and are nearer to Lucifer and Anti-Christ; and in
this gradation of wickedness those especially
excel, who from a greater and diviner power given

to them from God for edification, and not for
destruction, are more especially bound to exclude
and root out from the Church of God such most
evil destroyers. It cannot be, therefore, that the most
holy Apostolic See, to which by the Holy of Holy
ones, the Lord Jesus, has been given all sorts of
power as the Apostle witnesseth[a], 'for edification
and not for destruction,' can either command or
enjoin any thing so hateful, detestable, abominable,
and utterly destructive to the human race [as this]
or can make any attempt at such a thing.   For this
would evidently amount to a falling off, a corruption,
a misusing of its most holy and plenary power, a
complete departure from the throne of the glory of
Jesus Christ, and a very close sitting side by side
with the two principles of darkness in the pestilen-
tial seat of hellish punishments.   Nor can any one
who is subject and faithful to the said see in im-
maculate and sincere obedience, and not cut off
from the body of Christ and the same holy see by
schism, obey commands or precepts or attempts of
any description of such a character as this, from
whatever quarter they come, even if it should be
from the highest order of angels; but must of
necessity with its whole strength contradict them

* 2 Cor. x. 8.

and rebel against them.   On this ground, reverend sirs, I, out of the debt of obedience and fidelity in which I am bound as to both my parents, to the most holy Apostolic See, and from my love of union in the body of Christ with it, to these things which are contained in the said letter, because they most evidently tend to the sin which I have mentioned, most abominable to the Lord Jesus Christ, and most pernicious to the human race, and are altogether opposed to the holiness of the Apostolic See, and are contrary to Catholic unity, out of my filial affection and obedience refuse to obey—I oppose them, and rebel against them.   Nor can your wisdom take any harsh measures against me on account of this, because all my words and actions in this matter are neither contradictions nor rebellions, but the filial honour due to the divine commandment, as to my parents.   To sum up—The holiness of the Apostolic See cannot enjoin any but those things which are for edification and not for destruction, for this is its fulness of power, that all things may be for edification.   But these provisions, as they are called, are not for edification, but for most manifest destruction, therefore the blessed Apostolic See cannot enforce them, for 'flesh and blood' which shall not possess the kingdom of God 'has revealed them,' and not the 'Father' of our Lord Jesus Christ 'who is in heaven[9].'" Such was the famous letter[1], with which the Bishop of Lincoln, moved to righteous indignation at the degrading part sought to be forced upon him by the Pope, gave vent to the disgust and loathing which possessed him. Here, it is to be observed, is no revolt on Church principles. The Apostolical See is still the fountain of all sorts of authority; the Pope is still the representative of Jesus Christ. The revolt is altogether a moral one—a recoil from the awful abuse of this high office to the basest purposes— and a determination rather than yield to such an abuse to take a stand even against his principles themselves. Had Grosseteste's life been prolonged, it is probable that the revelation thus made to him on moral grounds would have led to a reconsideration, of his principles, and a clear perception that the sovereign power claimed by the Bishop of Rome was not only the necessary source of abuses, but in itself a gross abuse and unauthorized assumption, and that nothing more than the authority of a patriarch over a portion of the Church could be lawfully conceded to him.

[9] Matt. xvi. 17. [1] Gross. Epist. cxxvii. Matt. Paris, p. 870.

That light was rapidly breaking in upon him as to the true position of the Pope in the Church may be seen by comparing the language of this letter with that of the one given below, and more especially with his deathbed conversation preserved by Matthew Paris. But the moral recoil from the iniquities upheld by the see of Rome was already complete, and the bold and peremptory refusal of the bishop to install the Pope's nephew in the Canonry of Lincoln was at once reported at head-quarters. The Pope was transported with fury. " He could not contain himself for anger and indignation," says Matthew Paris, "with fierce looks and arrogant spirit he exclaimed. ' Who is this doting old man, deaf both in hearing and mind[2], who judges things in this bold and daring fashion ? By Peter and Paul, were it not for my natural mildness of disposition, I would hurl him to such a headlong ruin that he would be to the whole world a tale, an astonishment, an example and a prodigy. Is not the king of the English our vassal, I should rather say our slave, and can we not at our nod cast him into prison, and give him over to disgrace !' While these

[2] We may probably gather from this that Grosseteste had the natural infirmity of deafness.

things were said among the cardinals they
scarce were able to restrain the impetuousness
of the Pope, saying to him, 'It would not be expedient, my lord, that we should take any harsh
measures against that bishop, for to confess the
truth, the things which he says are true. We
cannot condemn him, he is Catholic, and most
holy; more religious, more saintly, and of more
excellent life than we are, so that he is thought
not to have a superior nor even an equal among
all bishops. This is known to the whole clergy of
France and England, so that our opposition would
not avail. The truth of such a letter, which has
now become known to many, perhaps, would have
the power of stirring up many against us; for he
is held a great philosopher, learned to the full in
Latin and Greek lore, a zealous lover of justice, a
professor of theology in the schools, a preacher to
the people, a lover of chastity, a persecutor of
simoniacal persons.' These things were said by
the lord Cardinal Giles[3] the Spaniard, and others
who were touched by their own consciences. They

[3] There are four letters of Grosseteste to this cardinal remaining. He seems to have been on friendly terms with him, and to
have given a prebend at Lincoln to a clerk on his recommendation.

gave counsel to the Pope, that he should wink at these things, and pretending not to see them, let them pass by, lest a tumult should be excited. And this they effected mainly because it was well-known that sometime soon the decease of the bishop would be likely to come[4]." The Pope appears not only to have been appeased by the cardinals so as to refrain from launching his censures at Grosseteste, but even to have made some apparent movement towards abating the abuses attendant upon Provisions. This seems the more probable account of the issue of Grosseteste's famous letter, but it was not the account usually adopted in the Middle Ages. The usual account is that given by Caxton in his "Chronicle:"—"This Robert, forsomuch as the 4 Innocent pope grevid the Church of England with taskys and payments agayne reason, he therefore cent unto hym a sharpe pistle. This Pope then gave unto a childe, a nephew of his, a canonry which fell void in the Churche of Lyncolne, and sent the childe to the bishop, charging hym to admit the sayd child. The byschop boldly denayed the resseyt of the child, wrote to the Pope that he would not nor should receive such to the cure of souls that could

<hr>

[4] Matt. Paris, p. 872.

not rule himselfe. Therefore this Robbert was summoned to appeare before the Pope and accursed. Then he appealed from Innocent his court unto Christ's owne throne. Then after the death of Robert, as the pope lay in his bed, one appeared to him in clothynge of a Bussop, and said to him, ' Aryse, wretch, and come to thy dome,' and after smote hym with his cross on the left side; one the next morn the Pope was found dead in his bed ale bloody[5]."

It is certain that, even if Grosseteste were excommunicated[6] he did not pay much regard to the sentence. He occupied himself as busily as ever

[5] Capgrave, in his Chronicle, gives a similar quaint account. " Roberd had be at Rome and pleted for the rite of the Church of Yngland under the Pope Innocent. For that same Pope reised many new thingis of this lond, and gaf the benefices without consent of the kyng or patrones or any others. And this same bishop Roberd wrot and said ageyn the Pope, and at Rome in his presens appeled fro him to the hy Kinge of Hevene. So cam he hom and deied, and in his deth he appered to the Pope and smat him on the side with the pike of his crosse staff, and said thus : ' Rise, wretch, and come to the dom.' "—Capgrave's Chronicle, p. 156.

[6] Mr. Luard (note to preface, p. lxxxi) says he can find no authority for Grosseteste's excommunication. But the Lanercost Chronicle says very distinctly, " In his last days he was excommunicated, which sentence he, being himself tenacious of justice, bore patiently and accepted, and also appealed to the tribunal of the Highest Judge."—Chron. de Lanercost, S. A. 1235.

with the great labours of his diocese, and with the affairs of the kingdom, and, instead of quailing before the Pope and apologizing for his bold speech, he addressed a public letter to " the nobles of England, the citizens of London, and the commons of the whole kingdom." " Would that the faithful and beloved children of the English Church and her noble pupils would mark the injury which that noble Church is receiving, that Church which is their mother, which has regenerated them with the Spirit, and with water; a Church which beyond all others in Christendom abounds in temporal goods, and has flourished in such a special freedom as to have been for a long time free and untouched by the impositions and provisions of the Roman Court, its goods not being exacted from it by the hands of aliens, but the inhabitants of the kingdom, its children, uniting to defend it. But now it is worn down and torn with so many oppressions and provisions, that while its own people are thirsting, it is compelled to give its milk (in grief be it spoken) for the use of aliens and foreigners, and its ample patrimony is ceded to the profit of a people whom it knows not, that patrimony which the pious devotion of its great men of old most devoutly gave for the advancement of divine worship and the support of the ministers of the Church and the poor of Christ; which now, against the will of its founders, is seized without reason not only by unknown persons but even by capital enemies, the inhabitants of remote regions, who not only strive to tear off the fleece, but do not even know the features of their flock, do not understand their language, neglect the care of souls, and yet collect and carry away money to the pauperizing of the kingdom. And unless a remedy be speedily applied with all caution against it, by means of these reservations, provisions, impositions, and processes of the Apostolical See, which through the too great patience of the English (I should rather say too great folly) day by day grow stronger, that Church which was of old free will be subjected to a perpetual tribute. Let, therefore, the noble knights of England, and the renowned citizens of London, and the whole kingdom take heed of the injury of their exalted mother, and rise like men to repel it. Let them see and understand if it be fitting and expedient that Englishmen (like oxen and sheep which bear the yoke and carry the fleece not for themselves but for others,) should behold others reap what they themselves have sown, and that thus those who labour the least should claim for them-

selves the food. And in order that by the abolish-
ing of this reproach of the whole earth, the noble
name of Englishmen, which, oh shame, has been
blackened, may recover its ancient title of honour
and with praise before God may be able to officiate
in divine things; and that the kingdom may become more powerful in adversity against the hands
of the provisors, and the attempts and conspiring
malice of the perverse, who have cast the eyes of
cupidity upon England, let the secular power be
effectually armed[7], that by excluding altogether
provisions of this sort, the priesthood of the
kingdom may increase in the Lord, and the treasure
of the English may be kept for its support; a
thing which indeed will not only tend to the un-
speakable advantage of the kingdom and its people,
to glorious title of praise for ever to be remembered, but also to an immense accumulation
of merits in the sight of God[8]." Here speaks at
length, and with no uncertain voice, the English
bishop, no longer the flatterer or the apologist for

---

[7] It is impossible, in reading these words, not to remember
how often Grosseteste in former years had denounced the seculars
having interference in Church matters, and how he had written
to the king, openly declaring that Rome had far greater claims
upon his obedience than he had.

[8] Gross. Epist. cxxxi.

Rome, but with a distinct perception of the rights of the National Church.

We have thus brought Grosseteste on his way from aiding and abetting Rome's extortions to denouncing them, from resisting them in his own case to organizing and encouraging a general war against them. His last words will carry us still farther, and show him walking at the end in still clearer light.

CHAPTER XIII.

GROSSETESTE'S DEATH AND CHARACTER.

1253.

Grosseteste's health gives way—He sends for John de St. Giles, as a medical attendant—He censures to him the conduct of the friars—Prophesies of the evils coming on the Church—His definition of heresy—The Pope guilty of heresy—The bishop sends for some of his clergy to hear his dying words—Solemnly condemns the Pope—His last words—His death—Estimate of his character by Matthew Paris—Character of Grosseteste—High reputation among his contemporaries—His lasting influence—In what sense a harbinger of the Reformation—The Pope's joy at his death— Stories as to what happened on the night of his death—His funeral—Miracles said to be worked at his tomb—Great resort of pilgrims to it— Efforts made to procure his canonization— Numerous testimonies in Chroniclers as to his merits—Example furnished by his career.

In the year 1253 Bishop Grosseteste, if we accept the usual date assigned for his birth, must have been no less than seventy-eight years of age. Yet, at this advanced age we see him giving the utmost proof of vigour, both as regards secular and religious matters. He was concentrating upon himself the attention of his contemporaries, more perhaps at this period of his life than at any other. Mens' ears were still tingling[1] at the awful denunciations to which he gave utterance against those who should impair the liberties of the country by the infraction of Magna Charta, and the bishop had taken up a position of almost direct hostility to the king. On the other hand his rupture with the Pope was complete. With no uncertain sound or stammering lips did the great prelate, who felt so deeply the responsibilities of the pastoral office, now give forth the expressions of his indignation at the way in which English benefices were sacrificed to Italian greed, and with firm and resolved spirit did he set himself to resist henceforward, without scruple or hesitation, this grievous scandal. We may readily conceive that such a position as this, which Grosseteste had now taken up, was an intense strain upon his physical powers, and that the natural infirmity of age rendered it

---

[1] This is the expression of Matthew Paris.

unlikely that it could long be maintained.   Grosseteste had suffered the usual penalty of studious
and laborious men in a weak and infirm state of
health, and in the autumn of the year 1253 overcome by his manifold labours, and the heat and
unhealthiness of the season, he fell seriously ill at
Buckden.   Immediately he summoned to his aid
his faithful friend, who had before, when he was
suffering from poison, so skilfully treated him,
John de St. Giles.   He was, says Matthew Paris,
"both skilled in medicine and also a lecturer in
theology, one elegantly learned and apt to teach,
so that from him the bishop might receive help,
both for body and for soul[a]."   To Grosseteste also,
he had another recommendation.   He was a friar
of the Order of Preachers, and as the bishop had
always made it the greatest point to have the friars
with him as assistants in his work while in health,
so in his sickness he would naturally desire to
have the same companions.   Yet the bishop could
unfortunately not gain unmixed consolation at this
period, even from the presence of his beloved friars.
He had already seen that zeal which distinguished
their first commencement begin to flag, and that
which proved afterwards to be the great bane of

<hr>

[a] Matt. Paris, p. 874.

their work begin to develope itself. "He gravely rebuked the Preachers, neither did he spare the Minorites, because that having been devoted to voluntary poverty, that they might not treat lightly the vices of the powerful, but reprove them with severe censure," they had failed to do so. "In that both you, John, and the other Preachers, do not reprove the sins of the great, nor lay bare their ill deeds, I hold you to be manifest heretics." It was these ill deeds of the great, both in Church and State, which were pressing heavily on the dying bishop's soul, and causing him to anticipate a bad future for his country. "He knew" says the historian—who though he often spoke harshly of him always appreciated the greatness of his character—"He knew in spirit that tribulation was coming on the Church, which we were not able to foresee. Therefore, he gave orders to the priests throughout his diocese, that they should solemnly, and without ceasing renew against all the violators of the great charters of the liberties of the kingdom, wherever there was an assemblage of men, the sentence of excommunication. This command was insolently opposed by certain courtiers, both clerks and laymen, who reviled the priests for carrying it out, which clearly involves them in the bands of the anathema[3]." Grosseteste, anxious to impress upon the mind of his friend John de St. Giles, and through him, on the Order of which he was a member, that there might be as complete an apostasy from the faith by moral ways as by impugning an article of the Creed, desired the friar to give him a definition of heresy. When John de St. Giles hesitated, the bishop proceeded: " Heresy is an opinion chosen by human sense, contrary to the Holy Scripture, openly taught and obstinately defended." And then he went on to apply this definition to the action of the Pope in the matter of benefices. " To give the care of souls to a child, is the determination of a certain prelate, chosen by human sense, on account of human and earthly motives. It is contrary to the Holy Scripture, which prohibits those being made shepherds, who are not suitable for driving away the wolves. It is openly taught, because in the sight of all there is brought a paper signed with a seal or leaden ball[4]. It is obstinately defended, because if any one pleases to contradict it, he is suspended, excommunicated, and a holy war is declared against him. He whom the whole definition of a heretic fits, is a heretic. But every faithful

---

[3] Matt. Paris, u. s.   [4] Bullata.

LIFE OF GROSSETESTE.   *Page 285.*

person is bound to oppose a heretic as much as he can. He then who can oppose him, and does not oppose him sins, and appears to be a favourer of his heresy, according to that saying of Gregory, ' He is not free from secret complicity, who will not oppose a manifest crime.' But the brethren, both Minors and Preachers, are specially bound to oppose such an one, inasmuch as both of them have by their office the gift of preaching, and by their poverty are freer than others to perform that duty. Not only do they sin if they do not oppose this, not only are they to be considered favourers of it if they do not, but as the Apostle to the Romans testifies ' not only they who do such things, but they who consent to them, are worthy of death[5].' It follows, therefore, that both the Pope, unless he ceases from this sin, and the said brethren, unless they show themselves zealous in opposing him, are worthy of death, that is to say, of everlasting death. The Decretal hath also said that for such a sin, namely heresy, the Pope may and ought to be accused[6]." As the days wore on, the bishop, suffering apparently from a low and wasting fever, felt all strength rapidly leaving him. The nights were long and wearisome to the sleepless and harassed sufferer.

[5] Rom. i. 32.   [6] Matt. Paris, p. 874.

He was afflicted "with a deadly lethargy and excessive weakness." Yet though his prostration was so great, he still strove to do his work to the end. It was in the beginning of October, three nights before the feast of St. Dionysius, that he caused some of his clergy to be summoned that he might impress his last words upon them, and also gain some comfort from their conversation. Again, he returned to the subject which was pressing so heavily upon his mind. "With a deep sigh he said Christ came into the world to win souls; if then any one fears not to destroy souls, is he not rightly to be called Anti-Christ? The Lord in six days created the universe, but to redeem man He laboured more than thirty years,—is not then the destroyer of souls to be held the enemy of God and Anti-Christ? The privileges granted by the holy Roman pontiffs his predecessors, the Pope that now is blushes not impudently to annul by this clause 'notwithstanding[1],' which cannot be done without manifest injury to them, for thus he is rejecting and throwing down what so many and so great saints have built up. What contempt of the saints is this! Rightly, then, shall the contemner be contemned according to that saying of Isaiah, 'Woe to thee that despisest,—shalt thou not be

[1] Non obstante.

despised[8]?' Who indeed shall preserve the privileges granted by him? The Pope in answer to this thus defends his error: 'Equal does not command equal, therefore no Pope can bind me who am a Pope.' To this I answer, 'To me it does not seem that there is equality between those who are sailing among the perils of the world, and those who are rejoicing in the security of the haven.' Grant that some of the Popes may have been saved. Far be it from me to say the contrary. The Saviour says, 'He that is least in the kingdom of heaven is greater than John the Baptist, although of them that are born of women none has risen up greater than he[9].' Are not, then, those Popes who of old time gave or confirmed privileges greater than this one living? Whence, then, this mischievous rashness of making void the orders of many holy saints of old? Although many Popes have afflicted the Church, this man has brought upon it a more grievous servitude than all, and has multiplied evils. The Caursins[1], open usurers, whom holy fathers and doctors have by their preaching caused

---

[8] Isa. xxix. 13.   [9] Matt. xi. 11.

[1] There is frequent mention of these Caursins, Italian usurers or money-lenders, in the contemporary chronicles. They seem to have preyed like a disease upon the England of that day; especially had they got in their clutches the monasteries.

to be cast out of France, and who had not before time troubled England, this Pope has raised up and protects, and if any one speaks against them he is vexed with losses and troubles, as was the case with Roger, Bishop of London. The world knows that usury in either Testament is stigmatized as detestable, and is forbidden by God, but now the merchants or changers of our lord the Pope, in spite of the murmurs of the Jews, openly carry on their business in London, contriving divers hardships against ecclesiastics, and especially against religious, compelling those who are in want to lie, and to affix their seals to lying letters, which is the sin of idolatry and the renouncing of truth, which is God. Again, I know that the Pope has commanded the Friars-Preachers and Minors that when ministering to the dying, whom they are to seek out diligently, they should urgently persuade them to make their wills for the succour and help of the Holy Land, and to take the cross, that when they recover they may wipe up their little property, or if they die, so much may be extorted from their executors. They have been accustomed also to sell those who have taken the cross, like the sheep and oxen in the temple, to laymen. I have myself seen a Papal letter in which it was inserted that those who make their wills, or who take the cross and agree to pay a subsidy for the Holy Land, shall receive as much indulgence as they give money. The Pope, too, has often given orders in writing to prelates that to such and such a person, an alien, an absent person, and altogether unworthy, who is neither learned nor acquainted with the tongue of the people of the land for the work of the ministry, nor intends to reside to exercise hospitality, they should provide an ecclesiastical benefice of a certain size and value, a very gross instance of which lately happened in the case of the Abbot of St. Alban's; and because a legate ought not to be sent into England except when demanded by the king, the Pope sends legates in disguise secretly armed with great powers. So many of these come that it would be tedious to repeat their names. Bishops also are allowed to hold a see without consecration, merely by election. The meaning of which is that they would have the milk and the wool without driving away the wolves and without even abandoning what they had before." The manifold abuses of the Roman Court against which the bishop desired to utter his dying protest came fast and thick upon him. The avarice, simony, usury, and cheating, the lustfulness, gluttony, vanity and worldliness which reigned in that court were present in sad array to his thoughts. "He kept striving to set forth how the court of Rome, trusting that ' the Jordan would flow into its mouth,' was ever striving with open gapings to seize upon the goods of intestates, and even of those who had clearly made their wills,—how to do this the more easily they have the king a partner in their robberies." " Nor," said the great churchman, uttering in his last moments a solemn prophecy, "nor shall the Church be freed from Egyptian bondage, save by the mouth of the bloody sword. That which there is now, is light; but in a short time, that is to say, in three years, heavier things will come." These words were pronounced with the greatest difficulty; the bishop's failing breath and utterance, the sobs and moans of those who stood around him and took part in the solemn scene, scarce allowed them to be brought to a conclusion. Hardly had they ended when voice and breath together ceased, the eloquent tongue was still, the zealous and earnest heart ceased to beat, and the great bishop went to receive his reward. "Thus," continues the same historian from whom all the above details have been taken, " departed from the state of exile of this world which he never loved, Robert, the holy Bishop of Lincoln, at his manor of Buckden, in the night of St. Dionysius. He was the open rebuker of both Pope and king, the censor of prelates, the corrector of monks, the director of presbyters, the instructor of clerks, the supporter of scholars; a preacher to the people, a persecutor of the incontinent, an unwearied exa‑miner of the various books of Scripture, a crusher and despiser of Romans. At the table of refection he was natural, refined, free, and polite, cheerful and affable. At the spiritual table devout, tearful and contrite. In his episcopal office he was sedulous, dignified, and unwearied[2]."

Probably few men have ever lived who acted more entirely upon principle than Grosseteste. Believing that the Church was designed by God to be the corrector of all human abuses, the censor and regulator of the State, independent of all human control, but charged with the most awful responsibility before God, he carried out these high principles fearlessly in his practice. As a chief pastor in the Church he claimed for himself, and exercised a complete and despotic sway over all within his diocese, admitting no rights of exemption from his authority, and acknowledging no civil power

[2] Matt. Paris, p. 876.

which could compete with his own. He scorned the notion of clerks being held amenable to secular laws, or indeed, of secular laws having any force save what the Church pleased to concede to them. These extreme hierarchical views led him for the greater part of his career to pay the most complete deference to the Pope as the head of the Church on earth, and to be ready without scruple or fear to listen to his commands rather than to those of the king or state. But together with extreme views as to Church power, Grosseteste also held the most intensely earnest opinions as to the obligations of the clerical office and the pastoral care. For a long time he strove to reconcile these deep practical convictions with the theory which assigned so high a place to the Pope and the Court of Rome. At length the manifest iniquities tolerated and upheld by the Pope produced in him a complete revulsion. From being in his view the representative of God, the Pope became the very minister of Satan. Once convinced of this, he fearlessly acted upon it. He denounced the Court of Rome and its evil ways, both publicly and in its presence, and to the utmost of his power in his own country and diocese. He called upon all men to resist its sinful abuses. He not only spoke, but acted. He refused obedience where before he had been all submission. He braved and must have expected, if he did not actually receive, excommunication. With all his strength and energy he advocated the solemn obligations that lay upon all to resist this Anti-Christian influence. His last efforts were directed to impress these duties upon those about him. His last words recorded these deep convictions of his soul. The most obvious characteristic of Grosseteste was his extreme earnestness. All that he did was done with all his might. Whether he were visiting, censuring, and directing his clergy, or dragging to light the abuses and scandals of monasteries, or contending with his chapter for the right of jurisdiction, or upholding the Papal claims, or again in turn opposing them, all was done with intense fire, zeal, and vigour. Hence it arose that many of his proceedings appeared harsh and tyrannical. When he saw the end clearly, he hastened towards it so rapidly that he overlooked and disregarded the means. He was not scrupulous about closely weighing and examining the weapons which were to produce a manifest and distinct good. Sometimes, doubtless, this reckless use of authority led him into acts of injustice. But the high and elevated motives which swayed him, must have been apparent even to those who suffered by his discipline. Matthew Paris, who shared the monkish prejudice against him, freely admits them. Others in his age, who were desirous of reform, seem to have thought that he did not go far enough. "Even Grosseteste himself," says Mr. Brewer, "needed the remonstrance of Adam de Marisco, when inclined to relax in his efforts[3]." Of his severity there can be no question; but to quote again from Mr. Brewer, "In an age, disorganized by the inefficiency of the sovereign, by the uncertainty and weakness of the laws, it is not to be wondered at that the sacred functions of the Church were disregarded, its spiritual character overlooked and despised[4]." Under such circumstances, a want of severity was sin. There cannot, however, be a doubt that Grosseteste was popular among his contemporaries. "Whatever hot words were spoken at the time," says Mr. Luard, "he seems never to have given lasting offence[5]." He so far surpassed his contemporaries in learning, in devotion, in courage, in distinctness of moral aim, in complete freedom

---

[3] Preface to Mon. Francisc., p. xc.
[4] Ib. p. lxxxix.   [5] Preface to Gross. Epist. p. lxxxviii.

from petty envy, that all, even in spite of themselves, were compelled to admire and reverence him. That he also attracted the devoted love of not a few attached friends his letters, and those of Adam de Marisco, sufficiently show. The attitude assumed by a man of the very great influence and power of Grosseteste towards the Pope, was in the highest degree threatening to the continuance of the Papal influence in England. He had already begun to call upon his countrymen for a general and organized resistance, to appeal to them on the ground of their constituting a national Church, which ought to be free from foreign control; and had his life been a few years prolonged, it may easily be believed that he would have been the leader in a general rejection, by England, of the preposterous claims of Rome. That this was ardently desired by many of the most influential noblemen, by the people, and by not á few of the clergy, who suffered most from Rome's exactions, is clear. But there was no man, when Grosseteste was gone, of sufficiently high and influential character, and distinct aims, to lead, and the paltry and shuffling nature of the king was a source of strength to Rome. The policy which prevailed, under some of Henry's more vigorous successors, the statutes of "Provisors" and "Premunire," limiting the power of Rome, were, doubtless, in a measure due to the bold utterances of the famous bishop, and in this sense it is not incorrect to say that Grosseteste was a harbinger of the Reformation.   Neither indeed is it altogether incorrect to speak thus of him with regard to the doctrinal points of difference between the Church of England and the Church of Rome, brought out at the Reformation.

It is true that Grosseteste did not formally impugn any doctrine taught by Rome, but he laid a solid foundation for the impugning of many. "We have seen," says Brown, "in this bishop, no small fruit come from the love of Holy Scripture.   From this alone he drew whatever noble protests he left behind him against the conduct of the Popes and others."   It was in this appeal to the law and to the testimony, in this entire submission to the voice of Scripture, that Grosseteste may not unfairly be called a harbinger of the Reformation, even though he may not have sided in any part with the views afterwards advocated by the Reformers, as distinct from those of Rome.   He, like Gerson and Savonarola, and many another man of noble, truth-loving spirit, helped to lay the foundation on which the building was erected.   That Pope

Innocent had a keen feeling of the danger to be apprehended from the open opposition of Grosseteste is evidenced by the unholy joy which he exhibited at the tidings of his death. Nor did this feeling of relief soon pass away. A year afterwards, when Conrad, King of Sicily, died, Innocent gave vent to a song of triumph, that now his greatest secular and his greatest ecclesiastical foe were both removed.

How far the Pope had actually gone in the matter of excommunicating Grosseteste must remain doubtful. It can hardly have been the case, as the Lanercost Chronicle asserts, that he was actually excommunicated, otherwise his funeral could not have taken place with all the ecclesiastical pomp which marked it. On the other hand, if we are to accept as authentic, the statement of Matthew Paris, that Innocent actually wrote a letter to King Henry demanding that Grosseteste's body should be disinterred and cast out into unconsecrated ground, it would seem that some anathema had been spoken against him[6]. Whether this were the case or no, it is certain that Grosseteste

---

[6] The demand is not grounded on the fact of an excommunication having taken place, but is told as a sudden outbreak of fury in the Pope, and as opposed by the cardinals. The statement is followed by the story of the appearance of Grosseteste by night to the Pope, his rating him in round terms for his audacity, and

in his death was regarded with the most affectionate veneration by his fellow-countrymen. Matthew Paris has preserved two stories, which throw around the departing bishop the grateful tribute of adoring reverence, and show that he was canonized and enshrined in the affections and admiration of men. The Bishop of London, journeying near Buckden on the night of Grosseteste's death, was said to have heard distinctly the sound of beautiful music in the sky, and two Franciscans, on their way towards Buckden on the same night heard, as they passed through a wood, the sound of a peal of bells, one of which was specially remarkable for its tone[7]. Honours, about which we can be more sure, were paid to him by some from whom they could scarce have been expected. Boniface, Archbishop of Canterbury, hastened to meet the body of Grosseteste, which was conveyed from Buckden to Lincoln for interment, and assisted at the solemnities of the funeral. Whether indeed the rapacious archbishop was brought there by a sincere wish to do honour to one whose greatness he might admire though he could not imitate,

inflicting corporal punishment on him, which nearly proved fatal to the Pope.—Matt. Paris, p. 883.

[7] Matt. Paris, p. 876.

or by an eager desire to seize upon the patronage
and revenues of the see during its vacancy, we
need not inquire too closely[8]. Certainly no more
fitting employment could there be for the Primate
of England than assisting in the funeral rites of
his most distinguished suffragan. There, too,
joining in the last honours paid to him in the
glorious pile of St. Hugh, part of which had been
reared during his own episcopate[9], were the Bishops
of London and Worcester, many abbots and
friars, and an immense crowd of clergy and people[1].
Grosseteste was interred in the upper south
transept of the cathedral where his dear friend
Adam de Marisco was afterwards laid by his side[2].
His grave was marked by "a goodly tomb of
marble, and an image of brass over it[3]," and very
soon the spot where the famous bishop rested
began to be celebrated for its miracles. To this
sacred spot pilgrims at once began to flock.

[8] See Matt. Paris, p. 878.

[9] Most of the nave, begun by Bishop Hugh de Welles, was
finished under Grosseteste ; and the Rood Tower—the most beautiful, perhaps, in the world—was raised as far as the upper
windows by him, it being afterwards finished by Bishop Dalderby.

[1] Burton Annals, Ann. Monast., i. 314.

[2] Pegge's "Grosseteste," p. 212.

[3] Leland, quoted by Pegge.

Richard, Earl of Cornwall, the second man in the kingdom by his birth and wealth, the friend of the bishop during his life, came to his tomb as to a religious shrine[4]. An infinite number of pilgrims resorted thither. A successor of Grosseteste granted an indulgence of forty days to all who would worship at the holy tomb[5]. A miraculous oil was said to distil from the marble, which could cure all diseases. One of the Canons of Lincoln was regularly appointed custodian of the tomb[6], and we may infer that his office was no sinecure. The miracles attributed to his tomb were so numerous that all the country came flocking to this source of power and healing. Yet it was not fated that this famous churchman, although exalted to the dignity of a saint by his fellow-countrymen, should reach the somewhat questionable honour of canonization by Rome. One who so freely and powerfully condemned the Romish system was scarce likely to be thus

---

[4] Burton Annals, Ann. Monast., i. 344-6.

[5] Bishop Dalderby, 1314. Pegge, u. s.

[6] About the year 1300 Henry de Beningworth, sub-dean was appointed by the chapter *Custos Tumbe St. Roberti*, in the absence of the master, Gilbert de Segrave; and an healing oil was supposed to have issued from it, of which John de Schalby, Canon of Lincoln, who wrote in 1330, gives an account.—Pegge, p. 213.

dignified. Happily the bishop's name was saved from this anomaly. But frequent efforts were made by his admirers to obtain for him this recognition, which in their eyes was of the highest value. John, the Roman Archbishop of York, to whom when sub-dean of that cathedral, Grosseteste had addressed an affectionate letter, was the first that applied to the Court of Rome for his canonization. In the year 1307 there was a general application to Pope Clement, and for the same purpose. The Dean and Chapter of Lincoln sent Robert de Kellingworth, one of their body, to prosecute the cause at Rome. The Dean and Chapter of St. Paul's addressed to the Pope a letter which still remains, in which they declare of Grosseteste that "he far surpassed all the philosophers of his time, and outstripped all theologians in divine knowledge and doctrine. His most famous works remain to testify this to scholars of our day, and by virtue of his genius, which was wonderfully strengthened with the divine grace, he was able to say, ' I have more understanding than my teachers.' But most of all did he excel in humility, simplicity and sanctity, so that he passed his life in innocency, chastity, and purity." His admirable performance of the episcopal office, the wonders which were revealed at his tomb are then recited, and the Pope is entreated to add him to the college of saints, and to allow him a place in the veneration and praises of men[7]. Another applicant likely to be still more prevailing with the Pope, preferred the same request. King Edward I., in a letter dated Carlisle, May 6, 1307, described the bishop to the Pope as "excelling in merits, illustrious for holiness of life, like the morning star in the midst of a cloud, like a candle not put under a bushel, but on a candlestick, that all could see his light[8]." At the same time wrote the University of Oxford in words of the highest eulogy of the bishop, and the Abbot and convent of Osency, where the bishop's discipline had not been unknown, joined in the request[9]. The king seems to have repeated his demand the next year, and another Archbishop of York joined in the general desire[1]. But all was to no purpose; the chastiser and censurer of Rome could not receive the imprimatur of Rome for his saintship, and the bishop's fame must rest on its own merits, without having the certificate of a Pope, to rely upon for its support. Happily it was able to dispense with

<hr>

[7] Wharton, Anglia Sacra, ii. 343.   [8] Wood, Annals, i. 249.
[9] Wood, u. s.   [1] Pegge, p. 214.

this prop. " There is scarcely a character in English history " says Mr. Luard " whose fame has been more constant, both during and after his life, than Robert Grosseteste. No one had a greater influence upon English thought and English literature for the two centuries which followed his time; few books will be found that do not contain some quotations from Lincolniensis, 'the great clerk Grosseteste[2].'" There is not one of the numerous Chroniclers of the day who does not mention him with commendation and reverence. " In his loss," says Bartholomew de Cotton, pithily, " the whole English Church suffers loss and damage[3]." A catena of passages containing laudations of Grosseteste would almost occupy a volume. The fame of Grosseteste as a great writer and scholar has long since died out,—his name has never ceased to be held in reverence even up to the present day. He has constantly been referred to by writers of ecclesiastical history as an early witness against Rome, although, very commonly, the nature of his testimony, the history of his opinions, and the special character of his life, have been entirely misunderstood. If the present volume has in any way

[2] Preface to Gross. Epist. p. ix.
[3] Chronicon, Barthol. de Cotton.

succeeded in giving a more distinct and truthful picture of him than has usually prevailed, it will not have been written in vain. His career furnishes a noble example to all who are called to the same high office, to which he was so entirely devoted. Working his way by the force of his intense practical earnestness out of darkness and error into light and truth; fearlessly and energetically striving to advance what he saw and believed to be right; without hesitation, compromise, or double dealing; with no selfish or worldly aims, but with a single eye to the glory of God and the good of souls, here indeed was a true Christian bishop, an athlete worthy of the strife, a witness for the highest form of truth, the supremacy of good over evil.

THE END.